The Twilight Pariah

ALSO BY JEFFREY FORD

TWILIGHT PARIAH

JEFFREY FORD

A TOM DOHERTY ASSOCIATES BOOK

NEW YORK

THE TWILIGHT PARIAH

Cover photograph by Roy Bishop/Arcangel
Cover design by Christine Foltzer

Edited by Ellen Datlow

A Tor.com Book
Published by Tom Doherty Associates
175 Fifth Avenue
New York, NY 10010

www.tor.com

Tor® is a registered trademark of
Macmillan Publishing Group, LLC.

ISBN 978-0-7653-9733-1 (ebook)
ISBN 978-0-7653-9734-8 (trade paperback)

First Edition: September 2017

For all my students.
Thanks for making me a better writer.

The Twilight Pariah

1

SHE PICKED ME UP at sunset in that ancient lime green Ford Galaxie she'd rebuilt and painted two summers earlier when she was into cars. It came around the corner like it'd busted out of an old movie. She sat there behind the wheel, leaning her elbow on the door frame. There was a lit cigarette between her lips. She wore a white men's T-shirt and her hair was pinned up, but not with any accuracy. Every time I'd seen her since we'd left high school her glasses were a different color. This pair had pink lenses and red circular frames.

"Get in, ya mope," she said.

"What's up, Maggie?"

As I slid into the front seat, she leaned over and kissed me. I gave her a hug. When I'd turned to her, I noticed out of the corner of my eye that there were two twelve packs of beer on the backseat.

"Are we going to a party?"

"No. Guess who we're going to see."

"The Golem of Arbenville? Russel Flab Cock Babcock?"

She smiled, took a drag, and hit the horn. We were on the road out of town, and I wondered where this meeting was going to take place, but I didn't ask, leaving myself open to the night. I'd seen neither her nor Russell since the winter holiday break. We'd been friends in high school, but each of us was now away from town most of the year attending separate colleges. I talked to Maggie on Skype maybe once a month, Russell, usually much less.

It was early in the summer following our junior year, and we were some distance along the path of going our separate ways. During a busy semester, dealing with classes and my current scene, I sometimes longed to be back in Humboldt Woods, lounging on the creek bridge, passing a joint in the heat of the afternoon.

"How's school going?" I asked her.

"Changed my major."

"That's like the third time since you started."

"I'm interested in something else now."

"What's that?"

"Archaeology."

I laughed. "That's a vow-of-poverty major."

"What, unlike English?"

"Bitch."

"Let's always be happy and broke."

"I've got the broke part covered."

"Are you writing a novel?"

"Basically, I'm dicking around."

"You need a plan."

"It's not the way I work. That's good for you. You're an ace planner. I take my hat off to you. I'm more . . ."

"Fucked up?" she said, stepped on the brake, and turned off the road. The car slowed, and I looked out the window to see where we were. We'd driven out toward the state park on a winding road through the flowering trees. It was only then that I noticed the cumulative smell of spring, a cool evening, a light wind. It was supremely dark, although if I looked up through the branches above the dirt path we traveled, I could see stars.

"You're taking me out in the woods?"

"Yeah, I'm gonna lock you in a cabin and put a gun to your head and make you write a book."

"Really?"

"Of course not. No one gives a shit if you write a book or not."

"Rough justice."

She patted my knee and the car came to a halt.

"Where the hell are we? I can't see a thing."

"The Prewitt mansion." She pointed through the windshield.

A ball of orange light came from out of the darkness, and after a few moments of my eyes adjusting, I could see that it was someone carrying a lantern. An instant later the behemoth form of the house emerged out of shadow and into the dim glow. Whoever held the lantern lifted it above their head and swung it back and forth three times. Maggie flicked her plastic lighter three times in response.

"Grab the beer," she said.

I did as I was told and she used her phone as a flashlight to illuminate our path. We followed the retreating lantern around behind the remains of the enormous wreck of a home. As little light as there was, I was still able to distinguish signs of the place's demise: shattered windows, shards reflecting back the lantern's glow, the leprosy of its three roofs, and a cupola that dimly appeared to have been bitten in half the long way by Godzilla.

"What's going on here?" I asked.

"Rot and degradation," she said.

We caught up with the lantern, which turned out to be held by Russell James Babcock, all-state linebacker from Arbenville High. He set the light down at his feet and came forward to catch me in a bear hug. "Greetings," he said, and squeezed me till my ribs squealed. I dropped one of the twelve packs. Russell was a good-spirited monster, Pantagruel with a crew cut. Last I'd talked to him he'd told me he was in perfect football shape at 320 pounds. If I remember correctly, he'd just changed his major as well, from business to something even more boring, like economics.

Maggie pointed out some overturned plastic milk crates a little farther back in the yard and waved us toward them.

Russell put his arm on my shoulder and asked, "Did she tell you why she brought us out here?"

"No."

"Wait till you hear this shit."

I took a seat, as did they, and handed each a beer. Took one from the box for myself and set it down. Maggie lifted a small glass jar next to her and held it while she turned her phone on and shone it at a pile of sticks and rotten logs that lay in the middle of the circle we sat in. She tossed the contents of the jar onto the pile and immediately I smelled gasoline. A moment later, she lit a match and tossed that after it. A whisper of an explosion followed, a whoosh, and then flames burst into life. Russell clapped.

We sat in silence and watched the fire. Finally, I said, "So how long are you guys home for?"

Russell was about to answer, but Maggie cut him off. "Let's cut the chitchat till later," she said. "This is what I've got in mind."

"Nice transition," I said.

"Check this out," said the linebacker, and nodded toward her.

"Okay," said Maggie, "ten feet behind you." She pointed at me. "There are the untouched remains of an old outhouse pit. I was here this week with a soil core sampler testing the ground. I know it's down there; I read it in the dirt I brought up. And I know it's lined in brick."

"A soil core sampler?" said Russ.

"We're going to dig out this old privy and reveal its hidden treasures."

"What do you mean by 'We're'?" I asked.

"The pit probably goes down a good ten or fifteen feet. I can't dig all that out by myself."

"You're just assuming we're gonna help you?"

She nodded.

"Tunneling through old shit isn't exactly what I had in mind for this summer," said Russ.

I raised my beer in agreement. "I'm digging enough contemporary shit. I don't need any of the old stuff."

"You're both helping me whether you like it or not. Really, Henry, you're sitting on your ass all day at the Humboldt House, guarding three dozen dusty paintings no one's wanted to see for decades and making minimum wage. And you, blockhead, you're over at the dairy farm shoveling shit in the mornings and working out for football in the afternoons. Not exactly what I'd call a tight schedule."

"Are you saying that's not work?" he asked.

"All I'm saying is that you two need to do something besides work for the summer. Something cultural."

"Which means me and Russell should spend our spare time digging you a hole."

"It's probably my last summer to see you guys," she said. "Next summer I'm going to Patagonia with this internship through school to participate in a dig near Quilmes. Who knows where I'll go after graduation? I may never see you again. Or maybe when we're really old I'll pass you on the street one day and we won't recognize each other."

"Jesus," said Russell. "Now that you put it that way . . . No."

"My parents are away this summer. The pool is open. You can come over and go for a swim after working out every day if you want. Deal?"

"Deal," he said. "But there have to be nights off. Luther's coming down once every few weeks for a day or two."

"Okay," she said grudgingly. "I can't really stand in the way of romance; I'd look envious. What about you, Bret Easton Ellis, are you in or out?"

"What do you hope to find down there?"

"We could find something really valuable. People have found all kinds of old bottles, watches, coins, dolls, false teeth, a wooden eye."

"We split the worth of everything we find?" I asked.

"Sure. I just want to experience what it's like and practice using some of the tools of the trade. Actual archaeologists would be pissed with amateurs doing this dig, but this place has sat abandoned for nearly a hundred years and no one's taken the opportunity. I figure Arbenville is pretty much nowhere, and this place is hidden in the woods at the very edge of Arbenville. Don't hold your breath waiting for a team of archaeologists to swoop in."

"I've got nothing else to do but write a novel."

"In other words," said Maggie, "you've got nothing else to do."

She and Russell laughed and I couldn't be mad at them. That scenario Maggie mentioned about us passing each other on the street someday when we're old and not recognizing one another stuck in my thoughts.

I lit up a joint and listened to her go on for a while about the wonders of unearthing the past. She was endearing but nutty, super smart and single-minded in her pursuit of whatever her current interest was, honest to a fault with everyone but herself. As for Russell, when he was playing football, he was a beast. At home, he kept a pair of powder blue parakeets, Charles and Susan, who flapped around him all day, perching upon his beefy head and shoulders as he sat on the couch watching his favorite show about hoarders.

There was another lull as the fire began to burn down, and I asked Maggie about the place. "You called it the Prewitt mansion?"

"That's all I know about it," she said. "I don't even know how old it is. I looked at it during the day, and it looks like it must be from at least the late eighteen hundreds, maybe early nineteen hundreds. I'm gonna have to do some research on it as context for any items we find."

"Seems a beautiful beat-up old place," said Russell. "I think I vaguely remember my mother or grandmother telling me something about it when I was small."

"I bet that house is full of stories," said Maggie. "Henry, you should write about this dig."

"Chapter one," I said. "They shoveled old shit. Chapter two: they shoveled more old shit."

"Do it," she said.

For the next hour or so, well after the fire had died down, we traded stories from the old days. Russell talked about the four weeks in senior year that Maggie was obsessed with the singularity.

"Do you remember that?" he said to me. "I had no idea what the fuck she was talking about."

"Torrents of obscure bullshit," I said.

"AI insurrection," she corrected.

Russell and I burst out laughing and she gave us the finger. "You're a couple of idiots. You'll see someday."

The breeze came up and I shivered awake. Through the dark, I saw the cherry glow of Maggie's cigarette. I couldn't recall where my thoughts had been, but time had passed; not a spark was left of the fire. I heard Russell whisper, "You gotta quit smoking, Maggs."

"Fuck off," she said. "I hope you two have shovels."

2

I WENT TO WORK WITH a hangover the next morning and watched the dust balls roll across the polished wooden floor of the Humboldt family parlor, noticed the wallpaper peeling in the study, and encountered an infestation of ladybugs in the third-floor bathroom. I dutifully guarded the paintings no one wanted to see, and slept for an hour after lunch on Karrick Humboldt's ancient four-poster, laying right in the spot where the wealthy old charlatan gave up the ghost. It was said the place was haunted, but I'd never seen anything in all the hours I spent there waiting for the visitors who rarely came. It was on the state registry of historic sites, and I was actually a state employee. That day, when I left in the late afternoon, I realized that I was the only thing haunting the place.

"How was work?" my father asked as I came in the door. He asked every day from behind whatever paperback he was reading. Science fiction, fantasy, or horror from the 1970s and '80s. He sat in the corner, in his comfortable chair, a standing lamp next to him. A cloud of smoke from his constant cig habit hung above him like a blank thought balloon.

"'Work,' in this instance," I told him, "is a state-of-being verb."

"Glad to see my tax dollars well spent."

"What's for dinner?"

"It's every man for himself," he said, and went back to reading. After my mother had died and he'd been laid off from his machinist job over in Milton, he'd retreated into near silence and the print reality of other worlds. Connection was tough for him and only getting tougher as he aged. Maggie asked me once if the reason I wanted to become a writer was to somehow make contact with him.

I put together a ham and cheese sandwich, ate it, and drank a beer. Went upstairs to my room and blew a joint out the window. It wasn't officially summer yet, but I put on gym shorts and a T-shirt and boots. A few minutes later, I was in the backyard, getting the shovel from the shed. Flat-edged spade or a pointed job? I couldn't decide so I grabbed them both. I went around front and sat on the curb, thinking about *A Midsummer Night's Dream*, the play we'd covered in my Shakespeare class before the semester ended.

A few minutes later, Russell pulled up in his SUV. I stowed my shovels in the back along with the one already there. As I got in, he said, "We're Maggie's pawns. If you could bottle her enthusiasm, we could initiate the singularity."

"We're the rude mechanicals."

He told me about his morning at the dairy, I told him about my haunting snooze in Humboldt's bed. We drove out of town through the twilight. It was going to be another clear, cool night. I tried to note what route Russell took in case I had to get there by myself sometime. He told me the tricky part was finding the path into the woods when it got dark. Just as he said that, he hit the brakes and had to back up to make the turn off the main road. The headlights lit the mansion.

"I think this place is even bigger than the Humboldt place. Looks like it must have been built around the same time," I said.

"Yeah, Magg told me that Prewitt was a politician of some sort. You know that's where the money is."

We got the shovels out of the back and went to meet Maggie. We found her in the glow of two lanterns, already in the outline of the old privy pit, digging away. She wore a red sports bra and a pair of loose blue pants with elephants on them. In addition to her red glasses, she had a Detroit Tigers baseball cap on her head. We were about five hundred miles due east from Detroit, and I don't think she'd ever watched a baseball game in her life. I noticed she wore work gloves, which was a good idea.

When she saw us, she said, "'Bout time." She stopped digging and leaned on the shovel handle.

"You look like you're doing just fine there," said Russell. "Do you really want me and Henry to fuck things up?"

"I need you," she said, pointing at him, "to shovel what I've shoveled out and toss it a little farther off. We don't want to have a giant pile of dirt right next to the hole in case it gives way and all that slides in on top of whoever happens to be digging."

"I hate when that happens," I said. "Exactly how safe is this?"

"Well, you know, for starters, what we're doing is against the law. That's why we're out here at night. You're supposed to have permits for this stuff. Other than that, this pit looks pretty sturdy. These people had money, and so their privy pit is lined with good brick. This is a real work of craftsmanship."

"Have you run into any old turds?" asked Russell.

"Just you two. Get to work. Henry, I want you to go through the dirt he tosses off over there in the new pile and keep an eye out for shards of glass or bottle caps, chicken bones, whatever. Once we hit a certain level, we're going to have to forgo the shovels and dig with trowels and finer tools."

We worked steadily, in near silence, with the exception

of Russell whistling "Somewhere Over the Rainbow." Maggie went at that dirt like a human shoveling machine. The big man was a little more relaxed, and I was downright lethargic in my search for shards of history. A half hour later, Maggie called for us to take a break. She'd gotten about two feet down into the six-by-five rectangle of the pit.

"Where's the top part of it, the wooden seats and all?" I asked.

"There was nothing but a few planks left," she said, stepping up out of the hole. "I broke all that up with a sledgehammer and dragged the remains back farther into the woods."

"Are we switching?" asked Russell.

"Yeah," said Maggie, wiping her forehead with the back of her arm.

"I'll go pit," he said.

"Henry, you toss the spoil dirt like Russell was doing, and I'll go through it and see if there's any signs of life."

"Will do."

"Russell, use the spade first and make sure the edges are done. We want to keep it level as we descend," said Maggie.

"Got it," he answered. "Hey, where's the beer tonight?"

There was no response.

A minute later, we were back at work. Both Russell and

I had been shanghaied into Maggie's projects before, and the three of us had gotten really good at accomplishing a task together. Once the digging started there was no more bullshit. If she was like a digging machine, Russ, now that he was in the pit, was like a backhoe, a veritable god of shoveling. For a long time my thoughts were occupied in dreaming up a story set in the old Prewitt mansion, which loomed above us. Then came the sound of the shovel head hitting glass.

"Hold up," cried Maggie, and Russell halted mid-dig. She and I walked to the edge of the hole where our friend, usually six-foot-five, was standing with his head at our shoulder level. Maggie jumped in next to him and called for me to bring her one of the lanterns. I did as I was told, and as Russell climbed out of the pit, she knelt and brushed the dirt away from the spot where the shovel head had landed.

"You see something?" I asked her.

"Yeah." She cleaned off the dirt stuck to it with her hand and held up a brown beer bottle, part of the label still intact. "It's a Schlitz. Probably late sixties, early seventies. I'm guessing we're gonna find a layer of them here. Kids probably came out here to drink and threw the empties down the poop chute. This was after the pit had been abandoned as a toilet. Russ, you switch with me, and I'll toss the spoil. Henry, you're up. Don't worry so much about these bottles, this is a foot or so from where the good stuff should start."

"The good stuff?" I asked.

"We'll leave the lantern right on the edge so you can see better. You'll notice when we're into the time when the thing was in use. You'll hit night soil."

"What's that?" asked Russell.

"That's actual antique shit turned to dirt."

"Does it smell like shit?" I asked.

"Get to work," she said, and lit a cigarette.

We must have pulled three dozen beer bottles circa the Summer of Love out of that hole. Schlitz, Piels, Miller, all the crappy beers my father drank when he was young. It was late and had grown colder. My muscles were seizing and my lids drooping. Russell had given up and was sitting on a milk crate drinking a beer. He'd arranged all the dug-up bottles around him like a private army. Maggie was still going through the pile of dirt with her gloved hands. I was surprised we'd shoveled that much in one night.

"How many thousands will these beer bottles get us?" asked Russell.

"None," she said.

My next weary thrust with the shovel made an odd noise. The metal head had deflected off glass again, but the sound was somehow different than the clink of the beer bottles. In an instant, Maggie was heading my way, waving her hands and calling for me to stop. I was more than happy to.

"Get out," she said.

Climbing out was a struggle. "We're gonna need a ladder soon," I told her.

She nodded, grabbed up a lantern, and jumped in. Kneeling and hunched over in the glare, she worked at something just beneath the surface.

Russell got up and walked toward us. "What?" he asked.

Maggie stood and turned around. She held the lantern out to illuminate the object in her other hand. It was a pint bottle of the most beautifully clear aquamarine glass, with a cork in the top.

"The thing was wrapped in a black cloth, and the material disintegrated at my touch. There are still some shreds, though. We should get samples."

"That bottle has a raised inscription," I said.

Maggie turned it and read slowly. "Dr. Anchill's Kind Nepenthe."

She struggled with the last word, and I said it aloud for her. "It's the drug of forgetfulness from mythology. It cures sorrow by wiping clean the memory of that which causes it. The phrase is from Poe's 'The Raven.'"

"Impressive, Henry," she said.

"Henry's like Wikipedia but with less personality," said Russ.

"Better than all that, though," said Maggie. "There's some Kind Nepenthe still left in the bottom."

I hadn't noticed, but when she shook the bottle, I saw about a half inch of dark liquid sloshing around. "I'll have to go online tomorrow and start looking into this stuff." She stood aside and held the lantern down at knee height. "We've hit night soil," she said.

The darker-looking dirt was evident even in the deceptive lantern light. It looked less dry, richer in texture. Just thinking about it, I spit twice. Maggie called quitting time. She'd constructed a top for the hole out of two-by-fours and a sheet of plywood so, as she put it, "Some poor bastard doesn't stumble in." We got the cap on, gathered the shovels and other equipment, and went to where the cars were parked. Russell and I wanted one more up-close look at the bottle.

I asked Maggie how old she thought it was.

"Probably early twentieth century," she said.

Russ turned it upside down and we watched the elixir flow.

The lanterns were extinguished and we were getting into the cars (I was riding back with Maggie in her Galaxie) when there came a loud crash from inside the house. It sounded as if it emanated from the upstairs, on the side that overlooked our work.

"What?" said Russell, and got back out of the SUV. "Did you hear that?"

Both of us, poised to get in the car, nodded.

"You want to go see what that was?" he asked.

"Fuck no," I said.

"It's probably some creature," said Maggie. "I saw a few raccoons around here when I first found the place. They're probably living in the mansion now."

"I'm picturing one with a cigar and a three-piece suit," said Russ.

Maggie dropped me off a little before midnight. I asked her if she wanted to come in and have a beer. She said she would and followed me in the back door. The kitchen light was on and I knew my father was still up. I saw the television light wavering in the otherwise darkened living room. I got beers for us and we went in to visit with the old man. He was in his chair, and we sat on the couch.

"What's up," I said to him.

He waved to Maggie. "Ventriloquist giant crabs is what's up."

"Sweet," said Maggie.

We watched a few minutes. During a scene in which one of the giant crabs used its psychic ability, my father, without ever looking away from the tube, said, "What are you two up to tonight?"

"She's got me and Russell digging a hole."

"Sounds healthy," he said, and lit a cigarette. The TV light cut through the smoke to reveal its swirls and motes.

"We're digging out the privy of the Prewitt mansion," she said.

That got the old man's attention. He looked at us and eventually laughed. "You know that place was abandoned when I was a kid," he said. "We'd go out there at night, light a fire outside in the back, and drink beer. One night we went inside and were breaking bottles, and I'm not exactly sure what it was, but something chased us out of the place. I remember the adrenaline rush and the running. It was right on our asses, growling. We ran past the fire and my buddy Nose picked up a burning tree branch and swung it at what was behind us. There was this earsplitting shriek and the thing vanished, leaving a sick smell of burnt hair. You ever smell burning hair?"

"What did the thing look like?" asked Maggie.

"I don't remember if I even saw it or not, but I was scared shitless."

"Sounds like one of your movies," I said.

He widened his eyes and smiled. "Could have been. Find anything in the pit yet?"

"An old medicine bottle. Some crazy remedy. Probably a mix of cheap alcohol and shoe polish."

"Any name on it?" he asked.

I was about to launch into my exegesis on nepenthe, but Maggie pinched my thigh. "I can't remember," she said, and that shut the conversation down.

Soon after, she said she had to go, and I walked her to her car. Out on the porch I asked why she'd pinched me.

"I knew you couldn't help driveling about the meaning of the name."

"What's wrong with that?"

"I couldn't stand to hear a story about a drug that erases sorrow in your father's presence."

"Why?"

She shrugged. "He was always nice to me."

3

WHEN I GOT OUT of work the next afternoon, it was raining, really coming down. I'd borrowed my father's car that day, so at least I didn't have to walk home. Good thing too, as my back and arms and legs ached fiercely from the shoveling. There was no way I was digging in the rain, so I figured it was going to be a night off. But Maggie called me before I made it the four blocks home. Meeting at eight at Russell's apartment. After I hung up with her I realized I could just bag the whole thing and beg off the project. Finding the old medicine bottle was intriguing, but nothing I couldn't have easily lived without. What was to stop me? Still, come eight p.m., I was knocking on Russell's door.

The Golem of Arbenville had his own place, a spacious two-room apartment over a corner convenience store owned by the local dairy he worked for. His boss, Ron Kerbb, the owner of the dairy, was an ex–football player. Pro or college, I had no idea, but he was pretty well known for it. He helped Russell out with a scholarship, a summer job, and a place to live just for the football fuck of it. He knew Russ wasn't going to continue with the game after college and didn't care. I was envious of the place for a number of reasons, but mainly because it was devoid of a gray, crusty life-form in the corner issuing clouds of toxic smoke and feasting on tales of wonder.

I knocked and Russell let me in. We wound up sitting in his living room by the front window that looked out over Arbenville Road. He didn't have beer that night. Instead he'd bought a bottle of cheap bourbon, and we drank it slowly on ice. It tasted like poison and I winced with every sip. Meanwhile the parakeets flew around us and occasionally set down on that crew cut like it was a landing pad. A Dean Martin record played in the background.

"How do you know which one is Charles and which one's Susan?" I asked.

"Susan's more laid-back," he said.

It took almost a half hour of prompting for him to get a parakeet—I think it was Susan—to squawk the line "Say hello to my little friend" from *Scarface,* but it did say it. I heard it distinctly. As it did, the door swung open and Maggie stepped in, soaking wet, no umbrella, carrying a briefcase.

"Where's your car?" said Russell.

"I wanted to walk in the rain. When it gets warm I go out and walk in the rain for hours. It's like you're living underwater."

Russell poured Maggie a shitty bourbon. She took a big gulp and launched into it. "Okay, so I went online and checked local and state property records and some other real estate investigation sites, went to the Arbenville library to see what they had on local history. I was going to talk to the town clerk, but I was afraid someone might wonder about my inquiry into the place, go out there, and discover our pit."

"What'd you find?"

She cleared her throat. "The place was built in the 1890s and occupied until 1923 by Prewitt and his wife. In December of 1923, Abner Prewitt, ex–district attorney for Tamblin County, died from a bullet to the head, fired from his own gun, by his own hand. The bank owns the property now. No one wants it. It's too far out from town and in too bad a shape. You'd basically have to clear the land and build again."

"You sound like a kid doing an oral report," said Russell.

"I'm being professional," she said, lifting the briefcase off the floor. She laid it on the coffee table and opened its latches.

"You were breaking our balls the other night about the jobs we had," I said. "Where are you working this summer?"

"I'm doing this," she said.

"Bankrolled by Mom and Dad?" I asked.

"While they're in Europe, no less," she said, and laughed.

"Some life," said Russell.

"Well, forget that. In any event, the wife stayed on in the place for a couple years after the district attorney died, and then vanished. Her name was Marlby—kind of a weird name."

"Is that it?" asked Russ. "What about Dr. Anchill's Kind Nepenthe?"

"Oh yeah," she said. "I found, in my search, a reference to it online in one of those ancient freebies on Google Books that's a pain in the ass to read in pdf, and a photo of an identical bottle on eBay, selling for seventy-five dollars. The Google page said it was a home remedy for melancholia. That was it. But about Anchill, he was actually a resident of Billard's Square, which isn't that far from here."

"I've been through there," I said.

"Me too," said Russell.

"In addition to being a renowned psychologist, Anchill was some kind of chemist. He'd worked in the early pharmaceutical industry, making medicines from botanicals. I got a sense from the Web that, in that field, he was well-known in his time. But I wasn't able to find a scrap that linked him to the Kind Nepenthe. It was probably a small side business he had." She reached into the briefcase and removed a sheaf of papers. One by one she laid them out on the table for Russ and me. Some were printouts of 1920s photos from the Internet.

"Anchill looks like Santa," said Russell.

"Prewitt's got prehistoric eyebrows."

"They say he was a real bastard in court, going after the death penalty whenever possible and sometimes when it wasn't. A hardass," said Maggie.

"What does all this mean?" I asked, sweeping a hand over the copies of old photos and real estate listings.

"So far, not much. We gotta keep digging, both in the pit and out."

Yeah, we kept digging, but now slowly with trowels and brushes and pans, and every square foot of dirt had to be sifted through a screen. Maggie had hand hoes and a small pickax thing she called a mattock. There was also a canvas roll filled with metal picks and scrapers and brushes. We nickel-and-dimed our way down through the years, through the dark night soil. The entire enterprise grew more tedious by the day, until about a week after we started.

That night was hot, and mosquitos made their debut for the summer. Maggie'd packed some DEET spray, but all in all that shit's pretty useless. It was Russell who made the discovery. He was at the bottom of the pit, a lantern beside him, scraping delicately away at the dirt. Maggie and I were sitting on the milk crates, taking a break, having a beer. The sweat was running off the both of us, and I'd taken my shirt off.

"If it's this hot now, imagine what August is gonna be," I said.

We heard a hoot from the pit. "My, my, my," yelled Russell. A moment later, he came tromping up the wooden ladder.

"You got something?" asked Maggie, and stood up.

I followed her lead and we both met Russell at the lantern that sat next to the opening. He was leaning over and examining something in the bright light. "Look at this," he said, peeling clumps of dirt off the thing. He turned his hand palm-up next to the light, and resting in the center of it was a small derringer pistol.

"Nice score, Russ," I said.

Maggie took the gun from him and put it closer to her eyes. "Wow. This might be worth something." She rubbed it with her thumb and found a name along the barrel. "It's a Colt," she said. "The handle's mother-of-pearl, with some nice swirly engraving. I'm guessing it's silver plated. It might be worth a hundred or two."

"So we've found a bottle of Kind Nepenthe and a gun," I said. "That almost constitutes a plot."

When it was my second turn in the hole that night, I

found a meerschaum pipe with a broken stem. The bowl had been fashioned into the head of a monkey wearing a crown. Later on, Maggie found the stem that had cracked off. She and Russell decided to bequeath me both parts of the pipe, so I might clean it up and repair it and smoke pot from it. I gladly accepted. As she handed it over, Maggie shook her head and said, "Henry, it's such a loser habit." Russell said, "Same as cigarettes."

That night, more stuff materialized from beneath the dark soil of the pit. A couple of plates, one broken, one just chipped. A cup and a saucer, perfectly intact. A folding straight razor rusted open. More bottles of various kinds, some in shards, some whole. A dark brown wig, half eaten to tatters. When Maggie found the last item, we heard her say, "Oh shit." She thought it was a body but eventually it became clear what it was.

Russell said he thought it was made of horse hair.

Not even an hour after the wig came up, I was down there, monotonously brushing dirt. Maggie said we were into "the heart of the past." I thought that was a beautiful phrase. If I'd kept a notebook, I'd have jotted it down. She also said, "Henry, at this stage of the game, I don't trust you with a trowel. Just brush."

"Where will I put the dirt?"

She went to her car and came back carrying a steel bucket with a rope tied around the handle. "You sweep it into the dust pan thing and then pour it into the bucket. Babcock will hoist it. I'll sift it."

Back and forth I swept with something that looked an awful lot like a paint brush you'd do the trim on a house with. I daydreamed I was applying blush to a dying woman. The closer she drew to the end, the paler she got, and the more blush I had to apply. Back and forth. I was at it so long, but when I came to, I was still pretty much where I'd started.

What I hadn't noticed at first was that in the spot I'd been working over, there was something protruding from beneath the soft dirt. It looked at first glance like a white weed sending shoots up toward the surface. I wasn't sure what I was looking at. I leaned in closer and then it became clear to me. Those three shoots were the delicate finger bones of a tiny hand. The initial sight was a surprise, but after that I wondered if perhaps it could have been the remains of a raccoon.

I brushed like mad, and what I swept into existence was a small hand, all five fingers intact and attached to a thin arm bone that disappeared into the night soil. "It's a baby," I whispered.

Someone back in history had thrown a baby down the toilet. I fled up the ladder, leaving the lantern behind, and went to sit on one of the crates in the dark.

"Henry, are you shirking your duties?" called Maggie

from where she was screening.

"You oughtta go see what's in the bottom of the hole," I said.

"What?" asked Russell.

"Henry, come on, quit being dramatic, just tell me," she said.

"You go see. But be very, very careful walking around. The lantern's down there. On the dark side of the lantern. Take your canvas roll of picks and brushes."

Russ joined her at the top of the pit. He held the ladder for her as she descended the nine and a half feet. She must have been down there for about five minutes when I heard her voice rising, ghostlike, from underground. "What the fuck?" she said, and I heard her repeat that phrase five times, each diminishing in volume. If I'd had my own car, I'd have been out of there. I'd as soon go home and sit with my old man watching *Attack of the 50 Foot Woman*. Maggie worked away for over an hour. In the meantime, I found her hoodie and robbed her cigs.

I smoked three, sitting in the night breeze, swatting mosquitoes. All of a sudden, I knew something was going on, because Maggie was giving Russell orders. Russell, for his part, was squatting at the edge of the hole in an uncomfortable-looking position. He reached out and steadied the ladder for her. He turned his body then, and I couldn't see from where I sat on the crate, so I got up and drew closer. In the light from the lantern below, Maggie appeared, inching up the ladder. She had something held close to her side in her left arm. When her knees were even with the top of the hole, she handed off whatever it was she carried.

Russell cradled it in his arms, and as he turned away from the pit and the light, I caught a view in half darkness of the complete skeleton of a baby. Russ leaned over the thing and looked at me with a grimace. "This is sick shit," he said. "Get the blanket out of the back of my car."

"Why?" I said.

"So I can put this creep show down."

I ran and did as I was told. In the meantime, Maggie climbed back into the pit and brought up the lantern. We set the two lanterns on either side of the light blue blanket, and Russ carefully deposited the remains in the center of it. It lay there like a skeleton floating in the sky. Maggie turned to me and said, "What the fuck?"

"We have to report this to the police. If we don't we can get in a shit ton of trouble."

"It must have happened a century ago," she said.

"It doesn't matter," I said.

"Well, if we tell them, then we have to admit that we were on this property digging up the outhouse pit. That's gonna be its own set of problems. What do they say about stuff like this in the archaeology books, Maggs?" asked Russell.

She knelt next to the thing and gestured at its head. "Did you guys notice these?" she said, pointing with two fingers of her left hand at two small horns protruding from the skull. The skeleton rested on its spine, but Maggie gently lifted its shoulder and pointed with her free hand at the backbone. "Ridged," she said.

"Like a little dragon," said Russ.

"And here," continued Maggie, pointing now at the bottom of the spine, where it turned into a short, sharp tailbone. "What is it?"

4

THE FIRST ONE TO speak was me. "Maybe it's a monkey of some kind."

"You know of a lot of monkeys with horns?" asked Russ.

"A genetic clusterfuck that resulted in a kid that looks like the devil?"

"I don't really want to know this," said Maggie, "but what I want to know is if it was dead before it went in the hole or not."

"Let's put it back down there and rebury it. Leave the place the way we found it. Think of all the bullshit we could avoid," I said.

"I like that idea," said Russell. "With all three of us shoveling, we could have that hole filled in in hours."

"I want to find out about it before I put it back," said Maggie. "If I get caught with it, I won't implicate you two, but I need to see this through."

"You're gonna take it with you?" I said.

"I'm going to put it in my trunk. Can I use your blanket for now, Russ?"

He nodded. "You're gonna drive around town with a baby demon skeleton in the back of your car?"

"That's right."

"How are you going to find out about it?" I asked.

"You know, look shit up, talk to people."

Russell held up his hand. "While you have the thing in your trunk, I'm not coming out here to dig. That's just asking for trouble."

"Agreed," said Maggie.

"I'm with you on that," I said.

"I promise, I'll leave you guys out of it if something happens."

We followed her to her car. She carried the skeleton and Russell went ahead with the blanket to lay it in her trunk.

"Watch it at the railroad tracks or you'll wind up with a pile of bones," I said.

"Yeah, yeah," said Maggie as she laid the thing to rest in the trunk of the Galaxie. We all took a last look at the creepy little guy, and then Maggie shut him in. "Will you two cap the pit for me and gather up the tools?"

We said we would. We waved to her and she was gone down the dirt road. It was while we were moving the plywood cap over the open pit that I heard a rustling in the trees and the sound of flapping wings. An instant later, the light from the lanterns was gone.

"Shit," said Russ. He took out his phone and hit the flashlight app. "Follow me."

"Both those fucking lanterns went out at the exact same time. What are the chances of that?"

As soon as the words had passed my lips, a strange sound came from above, like someone sweeping leaves on a wooden floor. We ducked and inched forward to where the shovels lay. I took the spade and gave the pointy one with the long handle to Russell. He was on his haunches, pointing the phone toward the sky. Something swept down from somewhere, cast a fleeting shadow, and clipped him in the shoulder. I saw him get hit and I saw him go over, but what I missed was whatever it was that hit him. The sound of it slamming him and the sound of it in the air made it seem solid, but to my vision it was a brief inkblot on a dark background. I helped him up.

"What is it—owls?" he asked as we ran.

We passed the spot where the lanterns had been shining not a minute earlier and discovered it wasn't that they'd gone out, but that they were gone. Nowhere in sight of the flashlight beam. I didn't even take time to say "What the fuck?" I just kept moving for the SUV, bent in half, with my head down. We managed to get there, put the shovels in the back, and get in. Russell immediately turned on the headlights.

"Owls," he said. "I've heard owls will attack people sometimes."

"Seemed bigger than an owl."

"They can get pretty big," he said.

Something moved in the treetops at the edge of the headlights' glow. There was a rustling of branches, and then that darkness-vanishing-into-darkness thing. "Did you see that?" I asked him.

"Yeah."

"What did you see?"

"I don't know."

"Me neither."

He turned the SUV around and floored it down the dirt road. It took me a few minutes to process the night. We drove along with some old music station on, playing Nat King Cole. Russell only listened to music from before we were alive. Finally, I turned to him and said, "What did you think of Maggie taking off with that dead baby in her trunk?"

"So weird."

"Do you think if she gets caught, we'll skate?"

He drove on for a while and didn't answer.

"So?"

"The thing I want to know," he said, "is what happened to the lanterns?"

The following afternoon, sitting on the southern veranda of the Humboldt mansion, smoking a joint, I wondered if what we'd dug up the night before was actually the skeleton of a baby. It just seemed so outlandish. *Maybe a prop of some kind,* I thought, but a prop for what? I called Maggie to see what she could tell me about it after looking the thing over in daylight. No answer. I tried to picture what it might have looked like clothed in flesh. The structure of the skull indicated that if it was a child, she/he had a kind of short snout, tending toward doglike.

Later, out on the turret, I tried her again, but no answer. I sent her a text that said, "What's the news on Baby Bones?" My phone was silent as I sleepwalked through the remainder of the afternoon. Just before I left to head home after work, I called Russell. He hadn't heard from Maggie either and had tried her more than once. He told me he'd be going by her place that night to take a swim after his workout and would call me from there and let me know if he saw her.

Instead of going home after work, I called the old man and told him he had to fend for himself for dinner. He couldn't care less. As long as there were enough smokes and enough dizzy old flicks on the box, he was sustained.

At the diner in town there was a waitress who I liked.

She was a college student at Potsdam. I'd talked to her at Christmastime for like an hour during a snowstorm when the place was dead empty.

Before going to eat, I stopped at the library to get a book out. It didn't matter what book as long as it was esoteric and I could understand enough of the jacket copy to bullshit about it for ten minutes. The waitress was into books, the more obscure the better. I think she was a philosophy major, but that was uncertain. What wasn't were her red hair and the cool tattoo of an owl on her forearm she showed me that afternoon of the blizzard. Beneath it were words, in a tiny, tight script formed into a feather—"The owl of Minerva spreads its wings only with the falling of the dusk."

I was just sliding into my favorite booth with a view out at the empty main street of Arbenville, and Sondra, the waitress, was walking toward me, smiling, pulling her order pad out of her pocket, when my phone rang. As she approached I put the phone to my ear and held up one finger to her to say I'd only be a moment. She actually sat down in the seat across from me.

It was Russell. "I'm at Maggie's," he said.

"Well?"

"The side door is open and it looks like someone, you know, screwed the place up. Pulled shit out and shit."

"Ransacked it?"

"Yeah."

"Where is she?"

"I don't know. I called into the house as loud as I could, but she's got the radio on and it's hard to hear."

"Why don't you go in and look around?"

"Should I?"

"You want me to come over, don't you?"

"How fast can you make it?" he asked.

I apologized to Sondra for making her wait. While I explained I had to go help a friend, she took the book on the table and spun it around to read the spine. "*The Decline of the West*?" she said.

"Oswald Spengler. You know, king of the bummers."

She lifted the book and handed it to me as I got up to leave. I took it from her and she gave this odd laugh. It was only as I was speedwalking the six blocks to Maggie's place that it struck me that her laugh wasn't a "Can't wait to see you again" laugh but definitely more a "You're so full of shit" laugh. She'd pegged me as a desperate loser.

I met Russell at Maggie's. He was standing at the threshold of the side door, which was wide open.

"What took you so long?" he asked.

"I was busy being an asshole."

He nodded as if that was a given. "You want to go first?" He waved his arm toward the door.

I stepped inside and he followed. Stuff was thrown

around, not so much as if someone was looking for something as just an act of mere vandalism or like there had been a brawl. A table was overturned, books and knick-knacks were swept off shelves, a standing lamp was knocked over. It wasn't all that terrible.

"A crime?" asked Russell.

"You mean the fuckin' music? Yeah." A tune by McCartney, repetitive, merciless lyrics and horns. I walked over and shut off the stereo system. We moved from room to room through the new silence, and immediately, once the old Beatle was gone, the situation went from annoying to eerie. In the kitchen, Russell found Maggie's phone. He knew her password and unlocked it. Our calls to her were there, but there hadn't been any activity on it since just after twelve thirty the previous night. Last thing was a call she'd made to an out-of-town area code.

"Hey, is the car out in the garage?" I asked him.

"Yeah, I checked," he said.

Maggie's folks were loaded, so the place was big. We searched the house, noting anything that looked out of order. Once we got past the living room it seemed as if whoever had the tantrum there had pulled it together and left the place in peace. Every minute in there was tense, though, like we were waiting for a ghost to pop out of a closet. At the back of the house, we finally came to Maggie's bedroom.

Jesus, what a mess. Russell and I knew it didn't take someone ransacking the place for that room to be in a state of chaos. It's hard to describe—books and magazines all over the place, small islands of laundry amid the other clutter—shoes, panties, beer bottles, Styrofoam coffee cups from the diner, empty silver cards that had held tabs of Sudafed, her favorite late-night buzz when she was working on a project. The place stunk like cigarettes, and her desk was piled with papers. The computer was on and the screen saver was a painting by Grant Wood titled *The Perfectionist*.

Russell looked around and said, "No wonder she wants to be an archaeologist."

That's when we heard a distant thudding sound. As if the house had developed a heartbeat. We looked at each other and froze. The noise continued for another few seconds and then died. Following it was a distant whispered sound, like coughing.

"You hear that?" I asked.

"Where's that goofy dog of hers? Chucky, whatever? It sounds like barking."

"Oh yeah, Shotsy."

We determined the source was the basement. The door to it was on the other side of the house, along a hallway that ran the length of the place. Before I opened it, I said to Russell, "You go first."

"Why me?"

"'Cause you're way bigger than me and if there's any trouble you can kick ass."

"Forget it," he said.

I finally opened the door, and we stood peering down into the darkness for a while. "If I was in a horror movie, I wouldn't do this," I said.

Then the noise came again. A pounding, the dog clearly barking now, and added to those sounds the cry of a voice.

"Is that Maggie?" said Russell, turning his phone flashlight on.

We plunged into the dark. I called out, "Maggie?"

"Henry," I heard, and that led us to a door in a small alcove behind a washroom bigger than my bedroom.

"Maggie, open up. It's us," I yelled.

"I can't," she said. "I locked myself in here and the lock jammed. You're gonna have to get a screwdriver and take the knob off."

I felt Russell's forearm on my chest, gently pushing me aside. His bulk moved into my spot and he put one of his sausage mitts onto the knob, giving it a twist. I heard something metallic crunching inside the mechanism, and then he pushed the door open.

"Are you taking steroids?" I asked.

"Of course," he said.

Light poured out of the room and momentarily blinded us in the dark. When my sight cleared, I saw Maggie, sitting in a foldout chair, holding a nine-millimeter Beretta in her left hand and clasping the little white fuzzball, Shotsy, on her lap with her right. The instant she saw us she lowered the gun and sighed. "I didn't think you guys would ever get here."

"What the hell's going on?" I asked.

"Let's get a drink, and I'll tell you," she said.

At the bar outside on the patio near the pool, Maggie and I sat on the stools and Russell played bartender. The only other time I'd ever seen Maggie so upset was when we found out in homeroom in our sophomore year of high school that Larry Detz had hung himself. He was a quiet, scrawny kid who was her first project assistant before she met me and Russell, when we were all assigned to do a group project by our science teacher, No Foolin' Doolin. Now she was as shaken and pale, slightly trembling. Russ mixed us up some martinis, two olives per toothpick. I kept waiting for her to spill the events, but she didn't. I finally said, "Come on, Maggie, what happened?"

"Got home last night from the Prewitt place. Made some coffee and put music on. I intended to spend the night online looking for anything I could find on the kinds of birth anomalies evident in the skeleton. Also thought that if I was lucky there might be news of the birth from back in the day. Through my university, I have access to the archives of local newspapers going back to the mid-1850s. Anyway, I never even got to the computer. I went in the kitchen to pour a cup. Set my phone down while getting the cream out of the fridge, and I heard this ungodly noise from outside. Like metal tearing. I went into the living room to see if I could hear it better, and instead I heard someone on the roof. There's two floors in the back part of the house, but the living room, you know, is only one story."

"Freaky," said Russell.

"I went into my parents' bedroom and got my mother's gun and went back into the living room. Shotsy started barking—she can't hardly hear shit, but she was going nuts. I figured, *Good, maybe that'll scare whoever it is away.* The next thing I hear is something scratching at the side door. The knob was jiggling and someone was throwing their weight against it. I grabbed up Shotsy and ran for it."

"Down into the basement," I said.

"Yeah, into that back room. Slammed the door and locked it. The burglar got in upstairs and made his or her way into the basement. I mean, they pounded at the door to that room and made the most pathetic whimpering noise. I almost opened fire to put whoever it was out of their misery. The whole thing wasn't right. I was so scared I almost pissed myself."

"You say it was a burglar. Do you think they stole something or were here to steal something?" I asked.

"I don't know. When we just passed through upstairs, from what I could see, it looked like everything was there. I'll have to take an inventory."

5

ONLY AFTER WE FINISHED the first round of martinis did I mention that we should call the police, but Maggie wasn't so hot on the idea.

"Somebody broke into your house," I said.

"Henry's right," said Russ. "What's to stop this dirtbag from coming back?"

"I'm a little leery of the police with the skeleton in the back of my car."

"We'll take it back to the Prewitt place and then you'll call them," I said.

She shook her head. "I'm not ready to do that."

"You're stubborn as hell," I said.

"You better sleep with that gun," said Russell.

"I've got Shotsy to protect me."

"The side door is broken open. Anybody can walk in."

"I'll call Albert in the morning and ask him to come over and put up a new one." Albert was a guy we'd graduated Arbenville with. He'd opted out of college to become a carpenter.

"What's your plan for tonight?"

"I've got you guys to guard me," she said. She pulled the Beretta out of her shorts pocket. "I'll bust a cap."

"I guess we're staying," said Russell.

It wasn't till the second martini was done that Maggie wondered out loud if maybe the person breaking in had witnessed us taking the skeleton out of the privy pit or was at least aware we'd been out there.

"Now that you mention it," said Russell as I switched my seat for his spot behind the bar, "somebody or something stole the fuckin' lanterns last night right as we were capping the hole."

"What are you talking about, stole the lanterns?"

"Yeah, all of a sudden the lights went out and we discovered on our way to the car it was because the lanterns were gone. Russ thinks it was owls," I said.

"What else?" said Russ.

"Fuck those owls," said Maggie, lifting the gun again. Shotsy turned in circles next to the pool and barked.

"You're making me nervous," I said.

"Agreed," said Russell, and she put the weapon on the bar.

By the third martini Maggie revealed to us that the last call on her phone had been to this guy who'd been her professor in anthropology at the university she attended. He was an adjunct, but he had an MA in the subject, and the bonus, as she saw it, was that he was interested in cryptozoology. She told us that she was going to take the skeleton to him to see what he thought it was.

"That sounds like a bad idea all around, starting with his interest in cryptozoology," said Russell.

"He's a Bigfoot kook?" I asked.

"All of that shit," she said. "Loch Ness, mammoths in Siberia, thylacines, whatever, but he's really smart."

I'm not sure how many martinis after that, when Russ was asleep on the blow-up raft in the pool and Maggie and I were in side-by-side chaise lounges talking almost from our dreams. I confessed my move on Sondra at the diner. She didn't laugh like I thought she would. She just said, "I'm over there all the time at night getting coffee. Sondra works the late shift a lot. We're friends."

I thought that was remarkable but I was too tired to respond. A few minutes later, when I was all but submerged, she said, "I'll tell her you're a good guy." That was the last thing I heard till the next morning when Russ heaved for air after having slipped into the water and nearly drowned.

I did the brave thing and called in sick to work, which meant that, since there were no scheduled visits for the day, the Humboldt House would remain closed. No tear would be shed, least of all by me. Russell begged off at work too. Kerbb told him, "That cow shit ain't going anywhere. See ya tomorrow." We took off around noon to drive the three hours to Maggie's university—me, Maggie, Russell, and the baby skeleton. It was a beautiful day, blue as the blanket in the trunk.

We wound up parking along the street in one of the seedier parts of town. When I got out, I could see the towers of the university about two miles distant. We were on a tree-lined street with a buckling concrete sidewalk. The houses were once-stately places from the time of the Prewitts. Now they were dilapidated, run-down by endless student and poverty-stricken faculty rentals. The one we headed up the drive toward was a three-story Victorian, painted a sink-cleanser green but painted without sanding to make the job a lumpy mess. There were patches where a slate blue was evident. There were patches above where the roof had shed its shingles. The porch wood was an unpainted gray.

We went to the back of the car and Maggie unlocked the trunk. Before she opened it, we all turned and looked around. The lid went up, and there was Creepy Jr. She carefully folded the corners of the blanket around it and lifted it to her chest as if she were holding a real baby.

"I hope nobody just saw that," said Russell. He closed the trunk with a slam as she headed for the sidewalk.

"Now look," said Maggie before she knocked on the door. "He's old, he kind of smells like a vase of dead flowers, he wears suspenders, and he doesn't say much unless he's lecturing."

"Can't wait," said Russell. Then she knocked, the door opened, and there was the old guy she'd just warned us about. He was thin as a rail, draped in a giant suit jacket and sporting a bolo tie with a silver clasp that was a classic alien head. No shortage of eyebrow hair, a straight line of a mouth. There was an aroma about him, like farts and chicken soup. He mumbled something and then nodded a few times as if trying to decide whether to let us in. Empty moments passed, but eventually I guess we made the cut.

Maggie did the introductions in the foyer. On first impression, the professor seemed okay to me. I mean, he was old—spiderweb hair, cracked lips and all. As we followed him down a hall to a back bedroom, he told us that he owned the house. "Unfortunately, it's not haunted," he said. He pushed back the door to the room to reveal that the walls were covered with pages from magazines and newspapers. Two steps into the room, and I could see it was all Bigfoot, coelacanths, and Mongolian Death Worms.

"Nice place," said Russell.

Professor Medley led us toward the back of Crypto-Central, pointing out, I assumed, some of what he considered his choicest inventory. He stopped at a cluttered table and from beneath a layer of crap pulled forth a big hunk of dirty plaster. With a bit of a struggle due to the weight of it, he held it out for us to see. "Impression of a fresh track from the woods just outside Ogdensburg, on the Canadian border," he said.

"Awesome," I said, and nodded, but I didn't see any footprint in what he held.

"Sweet," said Russell.

Maggie pointed out a plastic figurine of Mothman. "I saw the movie," she said. "That wasn't Mothman who kept calling Gere—it was his agent, trying to tell him to bail."

After a lengthy journey of diversions and lectures, during which we viewed Medley's own photographs of giant Native American skeletons, the egg of a supposedly living dodo bird he'd gotten through mail order, and a clear baby food jar that held a yellowing shot of jizz, or as he went on about it, "real ghostly ectoplasm," we finally came to an empty table and some chairs arranged around it.

"You obviously have the specimen in question, Margaret," he said, nodding to the bundle in her arms.

As Russ and the professor and I sat, Maggie leaned over the table and gently set the blanket down. She drew each corner back, revealing our treasure. "What is it?" she asked, and backed away.

Professor Medley squinted and took a pair of glasses out of his inside jacket pocket. He pushed his chair back with his legs and leaned over close to the skeleton. "Margaret, I'll need the muggles you promised," he said.

She turned to me. "Henry, you have a joint on you, don't you?"

"What are you talking about?"

"I told the professor we'd smoke him up."

"Why didn't you tell me?"

"I forgot," she said, and laughed.

I did have one in my shirt pocket I was saving for the end of the day, whenever and wherever that would be. I wouldn't be able to get more till payday at the end of the week. I lit it and handed it over to Medley. He nodded his thanks to me. Blowing big clouds of weed reek across the table, he inspected the baby from a few dozen angles, becoming more animated (which wasn't saying much) and slightly younger looking (which also wasn't saying much) as he proceeded.

"Interesting specimen," he said. I reached out like he should pass me the joint, but he completely ignored me. "You understand that what we're engaged in here is basically against the law. If the police come to me, I'm going to tell them that I instructed you to go to the police and turn this specimen over. For now, though, I'd say this is an interesting find. I've noticed the horns, the spine, the tail, the snoutlike nose. That this is a human of some kind is fascinating, but let's begin with the most fascinating

Jeffrey Ford

thing of all, and that is the very fact that this skeleton is completely intact. I mean, perfectly. Considering the conditions it existed in for near a hundred years, unheard of."

"So it is human?" asked Maggie.

"Let's check first," he said, "to see if it's made of bone and not some plastic or ivory. The thing is so well preserved I'm suspicious of it." He reached into his shirt pocket and took out a long hatpin and a cheap cigarette lighter. He sparked the lighter to life and heated the end of the pin till it glowed red hot. Zeroing in on a place on the left tibia, he stuck the pin into the bone and held it there for a few moments. Dropping the pin and lighter onto the tabletop, he then reached into his coat pocket and took out a jeweler's loupe and affixed it in his right eye. His upper body was resting on the table surface as he got as close to the leg bone as possible.

"It's not melted," he said. "So, we can rule out most artificial substances, resins or wax, etc., that would be used at the time." With the loupe still in his eye, he retrieved the lighter and illuminated the test area. "In bone, there are striations and pores. The color is less uniform than in ivory," he said. "This looks like bone."

"So it's real," said Maggie.

"I think so. If it was an ape of some kind that would account for the facial structure, perhaps, but the rib cage here is indicatively human, as are the pelvis and the arms and hands, with, of course, the exception of the sharp bone protuberances at the ends of the fingers. There's some difficulty in making a determination in the skeleton of one this young, but from what I see it seems the remains of a boy. It's frightening looking, but my guess is that these are genetic defects. It's surprising the child lived with these changes."

"I know there have been other people who've grown horns," she said, "but those cases are really skin tumors. These horns aren't coming out of the skin, but the skull."

"That is odd," said the professor. "There are believed to have been, in the history of humanity, a race of people born with horns. The Shining Ones or the Nephilim. They came to earth from heaven to have sex with human women. They were giants and gave birth to giants with horns."

"Do you think that's what's going on here?" said Russell.

"No, I think this is a case of compounded birth anomalies. Back in that time, if the child survived, it probably would have been rented out to sideshows as the Devil Baby or something equally heinous."

"Is there any way you can tell how it died?" she asked.

"No, unless there was, for instance, some obvious

damage done to the skull or a severed spine. Forensics isn't my forte."

"What is your forte?" Maggie asked.

"I'm afraid you'll never know," he said. "Now, how much do you want for it?"

"It's not for sale," said Maggie.

His expression changed and he, at first, appeared to be on the verge of tears, but what came out of him was a low, slow laughter. I thought his dentures were gonna hit the deck. He reached down and grazed, with his middle finger, the top of the small skull. "Come to think of it," he said, "there was a historical incident that's known today as the Devil Baby of Hull House." He sat in his chair and took a big hit off the last of my last joint. He dropped it, still burning, to the carpet and put it out with the toe of his wingtip.

"Hull House, in Chicago, was a place set aside for working poor and new immigrants to get education and important services. The program was begun in 1892 by two women, Jane Addams and Ellen Gates Starr. Addams, by the way, was later a recipient of the Nobel Peace Prize. The Hull House program became so popular and successful that a few years into it they had three different locations going and it was having a positive impact on immigrant populations, especially women.

"Then one day, at the main building, three local

women showed up at the door of the place and de-manded to see the devil baby. As Jane Addams later at-tested in an essay for the *Atlantic*, there was no such thing as a devil baby at Hull House. Somehow a rumor had got-ten out into the neighborhood since a child born with deformities had been sheltered in the building for a brief time. The truth didn't matter; the place was overrun for a month with people demanding to see Satan's offspring. There was even an urban legend concocted or repur-posed to fit the phenomenon.

"The story had it that there was a poor man whose wife had given birth to three daughters. When she be-came pregnant for the fourth time, he cried out that he'd as soon she give birth to the devil than another girl. Even though it didn't exist, there were reports and descrip-tions of the little tyke. Bright red and horned, leaping from one pew back to the next in the chapel. Skittering and slipping out of people's grips. He was malicious, mis-chievous, and sometimes deadly. Still to this day, it's said you can see him peering out the upstairs window of Hull House."

"But that doesn't have anything to do with our situa-tion, Joe," she said.

"Just trying to let you know there was some precedent for a devil baby. This legend was not confined to Chicago. For a while it broke out all over the place, mostly in urban areas and among immigrants. Jane Addams made the case that it's symbolic of well-to-do America's fears of the poor and the foreign."

"Do you have records of incidents like this?" asked Maggie.

Joe Medley leaned back in his chair and clasped his hands behind his head. His eyelids were nearly closed, as he was no doubt feeling the effects of my weed. "Probably. I'll have to look," he said. "It'll take a few days."

"Only ones from within the state," I said to Maggie. "It'll narrow down the possibilities."

"Good point," she said, and Russell chimed in that it could probably be limited to upstate at that.

"Let me know if you want to sell it," said the professor.

"Do you think it's worth money?" asked Russell.

"Probably," mumbled the old man.

"We're not selling it," said Maggie. "This is a child's remains." She got up in a huff and started folding the corners of the blanket around it.

"Sorry," said Russ. "I forgot, maybe because you're riding all over the place with it in the trunk of your car."

I laughed. And even Joe Medley gave a weak smile before his eyes closed completely and his chin rested on his chest. We left him there, lightly snoring, and showed ourselves out.

Back in the car, the baby stashed in the trunk, we

headed for Arbenville. It was a cool, clear twilight. You could smell real summer moving in.

"The professor is crypt-keeper status," I said.

"He doesn't seem long for it, does he?" said Maggie. "He's a cool old wanker."

"He seems smart," said Russ. "I can't believe he's so far into that 'I want to believe' crap."

"Even if it's not all real, it's still interesting," she said.

"How'd you like his Bigfoot foot?" I asked.

"It was like a piece of sidewalk," said Russell. "Did it look like a footprint to you?"

"I don't want to know where the ectoplasm came from," said Maggie.

6

WE GOT BACK TO Arbenville around dinnertime, and I asked Maggie to drop me off at home. I found my father sitting in the living room watching the tube. He didn't look over at me. He said nothing. I apologized to him for not calling to let him know I was going to be out all last night.

"Really?" he said. "I thought I heard you come in."

"When?"

"Late. I watched *Forbidden Planet* on TCM. It got over at around three."

"What exactly did you hear?"

"I'd just dozed off and then I felt a cool breeze and I heard you on the stairs."

"Did you hear me come in?"

He shook his head. "I meant to get up and go to bed, but I guess I fell back to sleep. I woke up sitting in this chair."

"You need to get out of that chair," I told him. "Sitting is the new smoking. You're going mushroom on me."

"Okay, I'll give it a try this week."

"What are you going to give a try?"

"You know, getting up and walking around."

"Get some air," I said. A few minutes later, when I left the room, I heard him light up a cig.

The next day at work, I was sitting in the visitors' area, staring up at the ornate ceiling and trying to picture in my imagination the scene of that weird baby being tossed into the shitter. I saw it at night. It was raining. The child was struggling in the hands of a burly-looking gent of the 1920s. Or what my conception of the 1920s was. He carried it to the outhouse held at arm's length. Even though it was dark, I watched closely to see if he threw the child directly in or if there was a moment's hesitation. I thought that would tell me volumes about the nature of the man and the baby. The child was screaming. He lifted it over the hole, and then the phone on the corner of my desk rang.

It was only the second phone call I'd received at Humboldt in three years of summer work. I lifted the receiver and I heard a woman say, "Go to the archives in the library and look for the daisy book."

"What was that?" I said, and the line went dead. I was a little stunned, wondering, What the fuck? I tried to remember the voice. To be honest, it sounded in some part like my mother's when she'd demand I do the dishes. It had a certain urgency to it also, as if my complying with the command was of the utmost importance. Still, it was controlled, clear.

I recalled that my predecessor, a girl from Arbenville High three years my senior, had told me when she was training me for the job that occasionally history buffs or teachers would call up and ask about some aspect of the house and/or the Humboldt family. She gave me a book to read on the subjects, *Humboldt Legacy*, like I was really gonna read it. I wondered if maybe it was that kind of call. Somebody was looking for the answer to something and they were going to call back later to see what I'd found. Kind of rude, though.

I took my ring of keys out of the desk drawer and set out for the Humboldt library at the back of the mansion. The place was as still as could be. Light slanted in through the high windows as I moved along the hall. The archive was a dust-covered glass case the size of a coffin on a mahogany base and legs that ended in lion paws. I expected the thing to be locked, but it wasn't. I'd never seen a soul among the few souls I did see at work there ever show an ounce of interest in it. From what I'd been told, though, it contained the mother lode of the Humboldts' paper records—photos, letters, journals, drawings—all in one place.

I lifted back the bulging glass lid as far as it could go, and the hinges squealed all the way. Things were arranged neatly, although a few of the stacks had toppled. Everything inside had a thin patina of dust on it, an indication that the glass coffin wasn't preserving shit. I was looking at a lot of brown paper and books, afraid they might come apart and disintegrate like the black cloth that had held the Kind Nepenthe. I started gingerly and then worked more quickly as I became convinced the documents wouldn't evaporate.

After ten minutes of digging and occasionally stopping to look at children's drawings and photographs of garden parties and a trip in the country in a horse-drawn carriage, I found a book, eight-by-ten with daisies embroidered on the cover. I opened it and found large photographs glued to every third page. The photos took up three-quarters of a page. There was one of Humboldt House, the steps and front entrance. Of course, the images were black-and-white, but they were in good shape. There was one of Karrick Humboldt as a young man. I'd know that blowhard anywhere. Smoking a cigar and wearing a boater. He was flanked on either side by young women. There were other shots of the homely Humboldt children, Carry, Bett, and Sands, each posing with the family dog on a snow-covered lawn. A wedding shot of the Humboldts, one of a car, one of the fountain back in the rose garden that's still there, still burbling.

Then I came to a picture of a young woman. She sat in a chair in a field of grass with a wood edging its boundaries. She was at middle distance, but I could still clearly see her face, just this side of pretty with a small birthmark on the left cheek. A dark dress and a white scarf around her neck, a drink in her hand. My eyes searched the photo, and I was about to move on, when my glance slipped down to the rest of the page beneath it. In pencil, in a neat script were the words "Marlby Prewitt June 1919."

After I saw her, it was difficult to believe she might be the mother of the devil baby. I took the book to the office and made a copy of the picture. As I was replacing the volume in the glass coffin, I heard a sound in the hallway outside the library. "Hello!" I called. There was silence. I listened more intently and heard nothing. As I was folding the copy of Marlby Prewitt to store in my back pocket, I heard the sound again—someone fleeing down the hall. My heart sank at the thought of a visitor, and I hurried to see who it was.

I searched the entire house but found no one. For the rest of the afternoon, I sat in the window seat in the northern bedroom on the second floor. The rain came down hard across the fields, and I studied the photocopy. My first realization was that I shouldn't have folded the thing up. The deep creases didn't help the view. The second thing that caught my eye wasn't her face, but down near her white shoes, in the grass, leaning against a leg of the chair was a bottle that, in its pear-like shape, bore a striking resemblance to the bottle of Kind Nepenthe. Could have been, but there was no real way to tell without color. The ramifications of the possibilities zigzagged in my thoughts all afternoon. I woke in the window seat close to dark and ran home.

I called Maggie to tell her about the photo, and before I could drop my bomb, she was off on an idea she had. She said she wanted us to go to the Prewitt place and check out the house for, as she said, "clues."

"That place is falling apart," I said.

"You can still walk around in there."

"What about the second floor?"

"Yeah."

"There's not going to be anything of interest left in that place. It's been abandoned for decades. Anything valuable is gone."

"What's valuable to the few is not always valuable to the many."

I laughed.

"I'll pick you up tomorrow night at dark," she said, and hung up. I never got a chance to tell her about the picture. I took it out of my back pocket and unfolded it. It was a little fucked up, so I laid it flat on my bedroom desk with a stack of books on top of it.

When I went downstairs to get something to eat, I noticed my father wasn't in his chair. I called him, but there was no answer. The bathroom down the hall was empty and the door was open, the light on. His bedroom, the same. I searched the house. I'd just finished checking the basement when the front door opened and he shuffled in.

"Where were you?"

He was heaving for breath and there was sweat on his brow. "Went for a walk like you said. Once around the block for starters."

"Really?"

"Death-defying." He landed in his chair with a thud and reached for the remote.

———————————

The following night, Maggie picked me up as promised. I asked her where Russell was.

"He's driving his own car. His friend's visiting."

"Luther?"

She nodded. "Did you bring a flashlight?"

"My flashlight sucks," I said. I turned it on. A pale imitation of light crawled through the darkness of the car.

"Pathetic."

Russ had bought a new lantern for Maggie to replace one of the ones stolen. We sat on the milk crates around its brightness. Luther and Russell had a couple of six packs of beer. Russ said he wouldn't go in the house without a few drinks first.

"I'm with you," I told him. He handed me one.

Maggie quizzed Luther to see what was going on with him. She and I had both recently met him at the winter holiday break. He'd been with Russell for two years. They were complete opposites. Luther was short and thin with long dark hair gathered in a ponytail. He had no interest in sports and wasn't half as earnest as his partner. His major in school was mathematics. How good he was at that, I couldn't tell you. Apparently, he was devoted to the game Dota. When I asked Russell what he liked about Luther, he said, "You know, he's sweet."

After we bullshitted as much as we could and drank all the beer, we removed the cap on the privy to show Luther what we'd been up to. Maggie opened the trunk of the Galaxie for him too and let him gaze upon the baby. I could see it took him a moment to collect himself upon its revelation. We'd all had the same reaction. Then he smiled and said, "Get the fuck out. That's not real."

We finally convinced him it was real, and then we had to convince him to go inside the house. Just before we set out in teams of two—me and Luther and Maggie and Russell—Russell said, "By the way, what the hell are we looking for?"

"Physical and/or psychic evidence," said Maggie.

"Evidence of what?"

I said, "She thinks she's going to find a letter in there, written by Abner Prewitt, saying something like, 'Had a rough morning. Threw the demon kid in the toilet.'"

"Henry, you're such a dick," she said. "Whatever you can find. Anything. Don't forget to knock for secret panels in the walls."

"What if I only psychically sense secret panels?" I asked.

"It's Vincent Price in the secret tunnel with the crowbar," said Luther.

"I hate all three of you," said Maggie. "Henry, for being a total asshole, you get to check the cellar."

"Fuck the cellar, I'll check it," I said. We stepped up onto the porch and stood before the black portal. I turned on my flashlight and waited. When the meager glow finally invaded the house it barely illuminated a patch of DayGlo orange graffiti that read, "Die!!!" The porch boards creaked beneath our feet, and an overwhelming mildew scent enveloped us like a cloud. Russell lifted the lit lantern at the back of our party and we entered. It felt like stepping into a mansion beneath the sea.

Not even the raccoons were home that night. The place was as vast and silent as a tomb. When Russell held the lantern up, it threw a soft green-blue light against the dark. The living room was devoid of furniture. The floors were bare wood, and the fireplace was full of glass from beer bottles shattered against the back of it. The million shards caught the light of the lantern and glowed.

"Try to remember any kind of interesting graffiti you might pass," said Maggie. "There's no telling when it might be from."

"I saw one over here," I said, and pointed to a spot near the entrance. "It was about Mr. Lace. Do you remember him?"

"Lace cut and paste," said Russell. "I wasn't sure if he was teaching us English or training us for low-level office work. What did it say?"

"It says he eats shit."

"They've got that right," said Maggie.

Luther and I decided to start with the basement—the worst place to have to go, but the one that might have the best chance of offering a clue. I didn't feel like going down beneath the rotting leviathan carcass of a house in the dark, and I was sure most other people didn't either. Fewer vandals would have ventured down there. Luckily, Luther had a much better flashlight than me. As we took the winding steps, he said, "What are we looking for?"

"Evidence, physical and psychic."

"Like?"

"That part's up to you." By the time we reached the bottom and stepped onto a stone floor, the darkness and what could be in it were getting to me. I had more than a touch of claustrophobia. Luther didn't seem to care at all. He lit a joint and passed it to me and moved the flashlight slowly, like a lighthouse beacon, over the stone walls and occasional shadowy piles.

"There's some junk here," he said. He moved closer to one of the gatherings of darkness and his light revealed it to be an old chair with once pink upholstery and wooden arms tooled to look like swans. "Nice piece," he said.

We moved on to the next pile, whose silhouette in the glow of the beam appeared to be a body on its back. It was instead a gathering of dry leaves. There were stretches of broken beer bottles. Then a beautiful old birdcage, three stories tall, made of bamboo—the front kicked in. Intermittently there were islands of old clothes. Neither of us wanted to get too close to them. The arms of coats, the legs of pants, a shoe here and there, imbued them with a sense of spirit. All of it was rotting, and the darkness of the place was enormous. There were pillars holding the house up, and always, no matter how far we ventured in, Luther's good light never found a western wall.

Another ten feet into the darkness and we discovered a tall wooden armoire, leaning back like a drunk against the southern wall. The carving on it was mind-boggling. Intricate woven branches of willow leaves. Above its closed doors, peering down across the still-intact front mirrors, was the face of an aged cherub. The luster of the wood was still beautiful beneath the dust and mildew. Our images in the filthy glass looked like a struggle at the center of an ice cube.

"I dare you to open that," said Luther.

There was something off about that cherub's face. Upon closer inspection, we noticed it had tiny horns protruding from its temples. "I dare *you* to open it," I said.

"Well played," said Luther. As he stepped forward to grab the two glass knobs, we heard a voice a distance behind us. It was Russell. I called over my shoulder that they should stay by the stairs, we were coming back. I wasn't sure if they heard me. I thought I heard Maggie yell something about a discovery in the attic. Luther pulled the doors open to either side and stepped quickly away. He lifted his flashlight and the two of us jumped because something moved in the armoire. I thought it was an animal with a dark coat—a cat or a giant skunk. My eyes adjusted to the beam, and I saw not a woman but the form of a woman, sitting with her knees pulled up to her chest. I thought I heard her weeping. In a heartbeat, she twisted into a dark cloud of smoke. The edges of her long gown swirled and her features blurred, rematerialized, and just as quickly blurred again.

The fog drifted out of the armoire, tentacles curling and unfurling like a slow-motion dust devil underground. I was stunned by the sight of it. She floated dreamlike and her face came in and out of focus like TV reception in a thunderstorm. The trail of smoke faded after a few seconds. "What was that?" asked Luther, and the living shadow appeared before him, solidified into a physical body, and raked a set of claws across his chest. Now it most definitely wasn't a woman but a thing with horns and a tail.

He screamed and I turned to run. It gave me a heavy blow across the back of my head. I went down face-first into the venerable dust of the Prewitts. It growled like a panther above me, and I made believe I was dead. A second later, there came the blast of a gunshot, and I knew Maggie and Russell had thankfully not waited by the stairs.

Maggie helped me to my feet. We ran over to Luther and found him on his back. He winced with pain and the flashlight showed the claw marks, his ripped T-shirt, and blood. Russell helped him to his feet. Maggie said she had a first-aid kit in her car. "Let's get the fuck out of here," I said.

We scurried back to the spiral stairs and ascended. Russell went first, with his arm around Luther. Maggie, gun still drawn, brought up the rear. Even with everything so crazy, I thought that she was a little too ready to shoot shit. But then we were running out the front entrance and across the porch.

Russell had worked a couple of years as a volunteer fireman in Arbenville's department. He knew first aid, so he did the honors. Luther, shirtless, sat on the trunk of the Galaxie, the lantern glowing next to him, while his wounds were cleaned and antibiotic was applied. There was enough bandage in the kit for them to be wrapped as well. Russell tied off the bandage and kissed his patient on the forehead.

Luther said, "That thing. It was there and then it wasn't there, and then, bam, it was there." Apparently, it had clipped him on the chin and knocked him on his ass before Maggie dispersed it with a bullet.

"It's a mix between the ghost of a woman and some kind of creature," said Luther. "It's both those things, though, simultaneously."

"I think I heard it growl," said Maggie.

"You definitely did," I said.

"Before you got there," said Luther, "it was in the armoire, crying."

"What I saw doesn't make any sense," said Maggie.

"Are we willing to call this a haunting?" I asked.

"I'm not even ready to call it that," said Russell. "That shit can't be real. Maybe there was some weird mold spore down there that was making us hallucinate. So we all thought we saw it but we really didn't."

"What tore Luther's shirt and scratched him?" asked Maggie.

No one had an answer to that one.

7

BACK AT RUSSELL'S APARTMENT, we finished off the cheap bourbon and everything else in the place. Luther, now in his partner's green football jersey many sizes too big, made a toast. "To Arbenville hospitality," he said. "You guys really know how to show a guy a good time."

"Hope you'll come back and help us," said Maggie.

"Did I hear you say you found something in the attic?" I asked.

"Yeah," said Russell. "Six boxes of empty Nepenthe bottles stashed in the dark back of the place where the roof slants down. There was moonlight coming through up there. Holes in the ceiling and puddles on the floor."

Luther asked to see the Nepenthe bottle, but Maggie said it was out in the glove compartment of her car and she didn't feel like going to get it. Neither did anyone else.

"I can show you what it looks like," I said. "Russ, you got a magnifying glass?"

"I do," he said. He got off the couch and went into the kitchenette.

As soon as I had the glass in my hand, I pulled the folded-up picture out of my back pocket. I had flattened it out, but it was too much of a pain in the ass carrying it around that way, so I'd just folded it again. Anyway, I spread it out on the table and said, "I'll see your discovery of Nepenthe empties and raise you one fine Humboldt House copier-,machine portrait of Marlby Prewitt, circa 1919," I said. Everybody leaned in toward the coffee table. Maggie gave a sigh of delight like a kid finding a pony under the Christmas tree.

"Did you come across this at the house tonight?" she asked.

I told them that I got it from the glass coffin at work.

"You don't think it's odd," said Russell, "that someone called you up and led you to the book that it was in?"

"Definitely odd," I said. "Especially the way the woman's voice commanded me." I admitted that I thought it sounded like my mother's voice. When I said that, my own voice got hung up and I felt a sudden surge of emotion. Maggie came around the table and sat next to me. I thought she was there to comfort me, but instead she said, "Henry, look at this fucking piece of paper. You folded it like sixteen times. You're a strunz. Why didn't you tell me about it till now?"

"I tried to," I said, "but you just hung up on me the other night."

"So what do you think of her?" she asked.

"She's an interesting-looking woman," I said.

"If you had to describe her in one word, what would it be?" asked Luther.

"She looks smart," said Maggie.

"Looks like she's got a secret," said Russell.

I handed the magnifying glass to Luther and pointed at the bottle leaning against the chair leg. He took it and grabbed the picture to bring it closer to his eyes. He nodded and then shifted his gaze back up to stare at Marlby Prewitt. "She does look like she's got a secret," he said.

We bandied about lame theories involving Marlby Prewitt and the ghost thing and the empty bottles of the elixir. None of it really made sense, and we knew we were just gassing for the sake of it because none of us ultimately wanted to deal with what we'd witnessed in the cellar. Sometime after two, Maggie said she'd take me home, and we said our good-byes. Luther would be going home the next day and wouldn't be back for a few weeks.

I was happy to have Maggie to travel with. I don't think I'd have walked home by myself. She must have felt the same way, because when we made it to my place, she asked if she could sleep on the couch. I told her she could, and we were in luck as the television wasn't on and the old man wasn't in his throne.

"Looks like my father packed it in early. You have the

gas chamber to yourself. Want a blanket?"

"No," she said. "I'm almost asleep. I just want to lay down."

As I was leaving the room to head upstairs, she said, "You should look around more at work. Obviously the Prewitts and the Humboldts knew each other."

"Yeah," I said, but the next day I did nothing of the sort. The memory of that thing we encountered still freaked me out. The silence and loneliness of the Humboldt mansion didn't help. I played music on the office radio and stuck to that clean well-lighted place, reading and staring out the window at the beautiful day. Around noon, Maggie called me.

"Henry," she said. "I'm at the library. I got a call this morning, after I left your place. It was Professor Medley. He said he had dug up an interesting tidbit from the annals of Arbenville in the 1920s. Did you ever hear of the Twilight Pariah?" she asked.

"No. Are you kidding?"

"There were these murders here in the late 1920s. All of them took place just after twilight. The killer was never discovered. The police couldn't tell if the victims had been slaughtered by a person or some kind of animal—a wolf, a panther, a mad dog. Nobody had a clue. But it was all centered around the wealthy community that existed out by the Prewitt place—the Humboldts, the Rirdons, the Websters, those kinds of families all suffered losses to the Twilight Pariah. Seven victims in 1927."

"Do you think this has anything to do with the skeleton?"

"I don't know. It doesn't matter. I'm into it anyway. But if I was going to try to convince you that there was, I'd tell you that family members attested to seeing a ghost come out of the twilight just before the victims were discovered torn apart."

"I can't keep this shit straight," I said. "So you're not saying it was the devil baby that attacked everybody."

"No," she said. "I didn't even think about that angle, I was just thinking about the thing last night. But really the thought of a baby crawling and mauling is ridiculous."

"I know. I was picturing the kid in a diaper, galloping on all fours across the front lawn of the Humboldt House, blood on his teeth."

"One of those to say she'd seen a ghost just before a murder happened was your own Bett Humboldt. Her younger brother, Sands, was disemboweled by the killer—his head nearly severed. See what you can find out in the archives there about it."

"This thing gets grimmer by the minute."

"Quit whining," she said. "We're close to something."

"It's summer vacation. I want to play video games and yank it. Hanging out with you is like an extra job."

"You know you love me, Henry," she said.

Against my better judgment, I left the perceived safety of the office and headed for the mansion library. I had to be able to look in Maggie's eyes and tell her I'd checked the archives. If I lied, she'd see through me in a second. So back to the glass coffin and its Humboldt smorgasbord. I looked through a lot of stuff, but most of it wasn't dated, and except for the Humboldts and Abner and Marlby Prewitt, I couldn't tell who anyone was. I saw enough of all four of them together to make the case that they knew one another well. But none of it amounted to anything. I gave up on the photos and went in search of more children's drawings. One by the doomed Sands was of an octopus with a yellow hat.

When I figured I'd been there long enough to be able to convince Maggie I'd been there, I began to tidy up the stacks of photos I'd gone through and happened to notice a small book, covered in fabric, bearing a print of African violets. I pulled it out from beneath a stack of paperback-size books. Inside that pretty cover, I learned on the first page that it belonged to Bett Humboldt. Beneath her name was the date—1925. It was her address book.

I stuffed the book into my back pocket and turned slowly to scan the room. I had an inner dialogue in which I convinced myself that not one living person on earth cared about a dead woman's address book full of dead people. It might as well already be dust, I told myself. By the time I got the archives put back together and closed the glass lid, I was fine with my theft. Back in the office, for the last half hour of work, I paged through it. There was only one name I recognized.

Forty-five minutes after I locked up the Humboldt place, I was sitting in the back of Russell's SUV. He was in the driver's seat and Maggie was next to him. We were parked on a corner in town back by the edge of Knight's Park. Across the road sat a big old place, only a little better kept than Professor Medley's house. There wasn't a light on inside and the sun was edging toward dusk.

"So this might have been her address way back in the day after her husband offed himself," said Russell, "but that was 1925."

"While I was waiting for you to come pick me up, I went online, found one of those address look-up sites, and I plugged in the address. They gave me the name of the owner of the house for $19.99. Marlby Prewitt."

"She can't still be alive. How old do you think she was in that picture you have? In her thirties? That photo was from 1919. She couldn't have lived past the 1980s."

"Yeah," said Maggie, flipping through the pages of the address book, "but maybe it's her daughter or a relative who owns it now. Somebody who might talk to us."

"I guess it's possible," said Russ.

"Are we going up to the door or aren't we?" I said. "I haven't eaten since lunch."

"Calm down, Henry. Let's see who's coming and going. See who's in there."

"I'm starving."

We sat there for nearly an hour, watching the darkened house. Russell told us about how he and Luther were going to get a place together after college. They wanted to move down to Brooklyn. When he finished, we sat in silence for a while, the windows open. Spring air swirled in, and up ahead along the sidewalk I saw forsythia bushes blooming. Night was minutes away. I was about to tell them how hungry I was again, but there was a sound from the house. I wasn't sure if it was a squealing hinge or the click of a latch, but I turned quickly to look. I knew Maggie and Russell had heard it as well.

In the slow, grainy light that was left, I might have seen a ripple of fog advancing along the sidewalk. It could have jumped like a big cat into the lower branches of an oak and scurried away through the treetops. It was almost a notion, but I could have sworn I'd seen something.

"Did you see that?" I asked.

"I heard the door open," said Russell, "but I didn't see anything."

"Neither did I," said Maggie. "What did you see?"

"I think I saw a kind of shadowy, blurry fog thing climb a tree."

They cracked up.

"I don't blame you," I said. "That's what I think I saw, though. Are you gonna knock on the door?" I asked.

"Not tonight," said Maggie.

"Are you joking?" said Russell. "We sat here all this time for nothing?"

It was less than a minute later that we saw a light go on in an upstairs room facing the street. I thought I could even see a shadow moving around in there.

"Okay, let's go," said Maggie.

By the time I stepped out onto the asphalt, night had settled. I quietly closed the door and met them on the sidewalk. "Do you have your gun?" I asked Maggie. She wore a cloth bag on a strap over her shoulder. She lightly patted the bag like it was a baby's cheek.

"Saints preserve us," I said.

"Why are you encouraging her?" said Russell.

We walked single file across the street, along the sidewalk, and up to the front porch. Maggie stepped forward. There was no doorbell, so she used the heavy knocker to alert whoever was awake upstairs. There wasn't a sound of response from the house. Russell knocked next. Still nothing. I went down the steps of the porch and backed up onto the lawn a few feet. The light upstairs was now out. I whispered to them this new development. Maggie went to the large window that looked out on the porch and put her face to it.

"What do you see?" asked Russell.

"Nothing," she said. I moved up behind her and looked over her shoulder. I thought I saw something white moving in the darkness but kept it to myself after the way they reacted to what I'd seen earlier. A second later an old woman's face appeared on the other side of the glass. It didn't seem as if she'd approached from a distance but more that she'd just materialized right there. Maggie gave a scream. I nearly shit my pants, and Russell gasped and grabbed his chest. The face was made of wrinkles. Those wrinkles were wrinkled. It was hard to read an expression, but the eyes were piercing.

We ran like nine-year-olds, jumped in the SUV, and split. Once we were in the safety of the car, we laughed our asses off. Russell said, "I wasn't ready for that."

"That face was the ultimate dried-fruit granny face," said Maggie.

"It hung there in the air like a washcloth on a hook," I said. "This whole thing is starting to scare the crap out of me."

"It's kind of all unpleasant too," said Russell.

"Where's your sense of wonder?" said Maggie. "Mysteries upon mysteries."

We wound up at the diner, and just my luck, Sondra was off that night. Maggie and I had coffee and Russell ate two hamburgers.

"I hope to hell that woman didn't see us," said Maggie. "I'm going back there tomorrow during the day and I'm gonna interview that old lady and see what she knows."

"Too bad I have to work," I said.

"Me too," said Russell.

"You two are a couple of fuckin' champions," she said, and tossed some money onto the table and left.

"She's pissed?" I asked.

Russell nodded and smiled. "Don't worry, she'll call us tomorrow and give us some orders, and it'll be just like any other day."

But that turned out not to be true. And it turned out to be especially untrue for Russell. I heard the news when I got to work the next morning and turned the office radio on. The local station interrupted an old Pink Floyd song with their "breaking news" alert, a series of what sounded like Morse code. I half listened to it while drawing a picture of the old woman's face we saw in the window the night before. I was getting carried away with the wrinkles, if that was possible, when it got through to me that someone in Arbenville had been murdered.

I looked up and focused my attention and heard that the victims were Ron and Alyssa Kerbb, the owners of Kerbb's

Dairy Farm. The farmhand who oversaw the early-morning milking had shown up at four a.m. He found the door to the Kerbbs' house wide open and their German shepherd, Woody, gutted on the front porch. Upon entering the house to see what was going on, he checked each room and came upon Mrs. Kerbb's body in the kitchen and Mr. Kerbb's body in the dining room. Mr. Kerbb was still holding an un-loaded shotgun in his hands. The police were, at the time of that report, unable to tell if the Kerbbs had been murdered or attacked by some wild animal.

I was stunned. I picked up my cell phone off the desk and called Russell. There was no answer. Next, I called Maggie, and she answered.

"Did you hear?" she said.

"Yeah. Poor Russ."

"I know," she said. "I went by his place, but he wasn't there. He's gonna be heartbroken."

Russell looked up to the Kerbbs and had treated them as his parents ever since his own parents had more or less disowned him after he came out in high school. The Kerbbs liked Russell's work ethic, his conscientious na-ture. Didn't give a damn if he was gay. Their dedication to him really made a difference in his life.

"I wonder if I should call Luther and tell him to come back if he can," she said.

"Don't do anything yet. He'll tell him, I'm sure."

"True. We'll wait and see what he needs."

"I hate to mention it now," I said, "but Twilight Pariah?"

"Don't think I didn't think of it."

The next few days were taken up with the wake and funeral, the investigation. Russell was called in by the police, as was everyone else who worked at the dairy or who was close with the Kerbbs. They were prominent citizens and there was an official day of mourning in Arbenville for them. Maggie and I had trouble contacting Russell. He wasn't answering his phone, and when we went by his place, the lights were on, but we knocked and waited for a good long time, and he never came to the door.

We finally caught up with him and Luther at the Kerbbs' funeral. As the crowd slowly dispersed following the burial, we walked along the path of the cemetery. It was a beautiful early summer day, not too hot. Russell apologized for not getting in touch with either of us. When Maggie gave him a hug, he started crying. To see his hulking form deflate in sorrow was a sad sight to behold. Luther patted his back. I stood there trying not to cry myself.

After walking a little way farther, Russell said, "It's that fucking thing, isn't it?"

"I wasn't going to mention it, but it really fits the bill," said Maggie.

"Is this more of that crazy shit you guys roped me into?" asked Luther.

Maggie told him about the revelation related to us through Professor Medley concerning the Twilight Pariah.

"But that was back in the 1920s," I said.

"No," said Maggie, "there have been other incidents over the years. I didn't get a chance to tell you all, but I got updates from Joe Medley. He identified more deaths along the same lines in this general area. The police never put the cases together because they were so far apart, roughly every thirty years. The later murders weren't as numerous, two or three instead of seven."

"I don't know about you guys," said Russell, "but I've got to get to the bottom of this now."

"Oh, I'm definitely with you," said Maggie. "I'm horrified that because we stirred all this up the Kerbbs are dead."

"You can't take responsibility for that," said Luther. "But it is an interesting question as to whether Russ's friends were killed because the Pariah is after you guys or whether it was a random murder."

"If it's after us, why doesn't it just come and get us?" said Maggie. She lit a cigarette and we walked off the path toward a fountain amid the gravestones. It was a place we used to hang out in high school. Now its white paint was chipped and faded, and the water in its bowls and pools was stagnant. We sat on the curling lip of it like we used to.

"Did you tell the cops anything about the Pariah?" I asked Russell.

"Are you kidding?" he said. "If I tell them that shit they'll put me away. Imagine trying to convince a cop about what we witnessed in the cellar of the Prewitt place."

8

THAT NIGHT, I STAYED in with the old man and we watched *The Brain Eaters*. At one of the commercial breaks, I said to him, "You know, lay off the walks for a while."

"What are you talking about? I can get around the block now without chest pains. I've got to keep at it. I'm ready to try two blocks tonight."

"Take a break," I said. "Did you hear about these murders the other day?"

"At the dairy?"

"Yeah. You don't want to be out at dark with that kind of stuff going on."

"Henry," he said, "I'm at the point in my life where I'll take my chances. Besides, if Jack the Ripper shows up, I'll fluff his cheeks." He threw a few halfhearted punches at nothing.

"You're the Chuck Wepner of Arbenville."

"We'll see who's laughing when I take it to him."

"They don't even know if it's a person. Could be a wolf or rabid dog or something."

"Whatever," he said, and lit a smoke. There was some brain-eating in progress on the tube, so he turned back to it.

A little while later I got up and went to the kitchen to whip us up some spaghetti and meatballs. His favorite and the extent of my cooking abilities. The meatballs were frozen and the rest, boiling water and heating sauce, I had down like a champ. Thirty minutes later, when I came back into the living room, he wasn't in his chair. I set the food on the tray he kept next to his chair and called down the hall to see if he was in the bathroom. No answer. I found the inside front door open and the screen door unlocked.

I went out into the night and looked up and down the street. There were lit streetlamps every fifty feet or so, and I could see fairly well in either direction, but I didn't see his hulking silhouette anywhere. "Bullshit," I said, and started off at a jog toward the west. I had no idea what direction he'd gone in or what he'd meant earlier by doing two blocks. I got around the corner and was out of breath. Looked up ahead of me and saw no one. Started jogging again, but the streets were empty. When I arrived at the end of that block, there was another decision to make. I went right and around the corner. Way down the street, I could barely make out a figure moving.

After sprinting twenty yards, I figured I was better off walking fast, which I did. I gained on the shadow. When I'd closed the distance between us by half, I yelled, "Dad!" The figure stopped under a streetlight and turned, but it wasn't my father. It was a woman. I jogged again to catch up with her. I thought maybe she might have passed him. When I drew a little closer, I saw it was Sondra from the diner.

As I approached, she said, "It's you. Did you just call me *Dad*?"

I gave a half-assed laugh and told her I was looking for my father.

"Does he look like Oswald Spengler?" she asked.

I just shook my head and grinned stupidly.

"How come you don't come to the diner and talk to me anymore?" she asked.

"I was there the other night."

"I'm heading to work right now. I'm just doing a short shift. I get off at midnight. Come over and have some coffee. It usually isn't busy this time during the week." She smiled at me, and not the "you're a loser" smile. "Hope you find your father."

"Thanks," I said, and turned to run back home. After speaking with Sondra, I had all kinds of energy and flew the distance to the house without losing my breath at all. Of course, the old man was sitting at his tray in the living room, finishing off a plate of spaghetti. "Great meatballs!" he said.

I was pissed at him, but if he hadn't gone out I'd not have run into Sondra. I told him I was worried about him, a ploy to get him to lend me his car, and it worked. I scarfed down some dinner, went upstairs, showered and shaved and dressed in something other than sweatpants and a ripped T-shirt. As I was on the way out the door, I got a phone call. It was Maggie.

"No fucking way," I said to myself, and let it ring through to voice mail. I got in the car and started it. But before I put the car in gear, I got weak and called her back. When she answered, I said, "What?"

"Meet me at the diner in a few minutes. Joe Medley is with me. He brought some weapons for us."

"I'm headed there now," I said. There was no way out of it. They'd see me if I tried to sneak in and only talk to Sondra. I was trapped. A few minutes later, I was standing next to the booth holding Maggie on one side and Professor Medley on the other. I sat next to Maggie. She put her finger to her lips and made a motion for me to get closer.

Joe leaned forward and reached into his inside jacket pocket. He brought forth, clasped between his index and middle fingers, a joint in red paper. "First things first," he said. He handed me the joint and said, "Thanks." The surprise of it made me laugh out loud. I took it and stashed it in my shirt pocket.

"A weapon unto itself," he said.

The waitress came to take our order, but it wasn't who I was expecting to see. While Joe and Maggie told her what they wanted, I looked around the place to see if I could spot Sondra. There weren't that many people there and our waitress seemed to be handling the entire place. There was a small room in the back that had two or three tables in it that I couldn't readily see from where I sat. I could have easily gotten up and looked, but I didn't want to make a spectacle of myself. So I stayed put and listened to Joe.

"Okay . . . okay . . . I've got three weapons for you. Each of these is supposed to have been proven to be reliably effective."

"By who?" I asked.

The professor looked at me and squinted. "Would you like the actual names of people you'll have no way of identifying and know nothing about, or specific incidents that no matter how corroborated you'll doubt?"

Served by Professor Medley, I beheld the weapons he'd brought. Each from a different pocket of his boxy jacket. He laid them out slowly in a row. A see-through plastic bag with, it looked like, sugar or salt in it. A bag of lawn clippings? And a bag of dried white rice. Maggie and I looked at each other and laughed.

"What's this one for?" I asked, pointing at the bag of rice. "In case you run into a ghost wedding?"

Maggie got herself under control and pushed me back as she sat forward. "Go ahead, Joe," she said. "I'm into it."

There was no stopping Joe. He started with the grass clippings, which was actually a bag of four different herbs. "You've got five-finger grass, the leaves of the ox-eye daisy, mullein, and ass's foot. You take some of this and toss it in the air in front of you or wherever the spirit manifests. The aromas and the properties of the different herbs sifting down to the ground will confuse the spirit. Ideal for a quick getaway."

"You're going to take on that thing that gashed Luther with a bag of ass foot?" I said.

"Ass's foot," the professor corrected. "Next, we have a bag of salt. Salt is probably one of the earliest magical substances known to humanity. Salt preserves in the physical world and destroys in the spiritual world. And last is a bag of rice. This technique has long been known to work against spirits throughout the world. If accosted by a malevolent spirit, you empty a bag of rice onto the floor. When something like rice or acorns or anything small and in a large number like that has been spilled, it is incumbent upon a spirit to pick each and every morsel up before continuing to haunt. Voilà."

"It's incumbent upon the spirit?" I said.

"The knowledge these methods have been derived from," said the professor, "predates the modern world. Their use has remained alive over millennia."

"Your point?" I asked.

"There is more in heaven and earth, Horatio . . ."

"Henry, shut up," said Maggie. "This is it, Joe? There's no kind of spirit-killer gun or anything like that? I mean, I shot at the thing and it vanished."

"Probably more so from the sound than the bullet. You can't kill the dead. You've got to outsmart them."

"Okay," I said. "I'll take the rice." I grabbed the bag and put it in my shirt pocket.

"I'm going with the salt," said Maggie, and she took that one.

"We're stiffing Russell with the grass clippings?" I asked.

Maggie laughed and took the herbs for our friend. "And poor Luther's got only his good looks."

"You've got the fucking gun," I said. "You should give him the salt."

She agreed. Our meeting with Joe went on for a while more and he filled us in on the grisly details of the Twilight Pariah murders—depth of wounds, the severing of tendons, the breaking of bones, the slicing off of faces.

Still, he had no answers as to who or what had committed the murders. In each historical instance when the killer struck, the police eventually put the savagery off to wild animal attacks because there was no suspect and no motive. The most likely candidate in each case was thought to be an Eastern cougar, which can grow to more than two hundred pounds.

Joe had to take off and head home. He'd just been passing through on his way back from a cryptozoology conference in Albany. He told us to contact him if we found any more information. I was left with Maggie. We ordered one more cup of coffee.

"Jeez, I'm sorry I ever got us started on this thing," she said.

"Well, someone really needs to go to the cops and explain what's going on."

"What's to explain? We don't know whether what we encountered killed Kerbb and his wife or not."

"I'm having all kinds of creepy thoughts."

She got up to leave and asked me if I wanted a ride. I told her I had been originally going to the diner to talk to Sondra while she was on her shift.

"I haven't seen her," said Maggie.

"What are you doing now?"

"Albert's coming over my house tonight. We're going to hang out and have a few drinks."

"The carpenter?" I said.

"He's hot. I need some distraction."

The next morning, when I came down for breakfast, my father told me, "I should have listened to you last night. Only about two blocks away, they found some local girl sliced up, her tongue and eyes missing." He turned the newspaper around for me to see the headline. **Potsdam Student Found Murdered on Lark Street.** I was stunned—couldn't breathe, swallow.

"Did you know her?" asked the old man. His finger tapped a photo of Sondra beneath the headline where the paper was folded in half.

I sat down at the breakfast table. "No."

"Seems like walking's the new smoking," he said.

I showered, shaved, went to work in a complete daze. After having listened to Joe recount the horrors of the Twilight Pariah killings at the diner, my mind concocted the most brutal images of poor Sondra. I felt completely guilty and spent the entire morning staring out the third-story parlor window, thinking how I should go about confessing. The only thing that woke me from that morbid trance was the sound of someone calling me downstairs. I froze with fear as the name, *Henry*, came rising from below. On the fourth repetition, I recognized it was Russell's voice.

I found him in the library, with Maggie and Luther. When I walked through the door, Maggie said, "Did you see about Sondra?"

I could only nod, afraid my voice would crack and I'd start bawling.

"Ditch this and let's go see that old woman," said Russell.

"Let me lock up," I said.

———————

It was almost one o'clock in the afternoon when we pulled up across the street fifty yards away from the old house. Russell parked and we sat there for a while.

"What I don't understand," said Luther, "is why the thing only goes after people you guys know and doesn't come after you. It's clear we can't stop it."

"I can't figure that out," said Maggie. "Who's coming in with me?"

"I'm definitely going," said Russell. He'd seemed ready to beat something to death since the news of the Kerbbs had sunk in. It was probably thanks to Luther that the genie wasn't out of the bottle . . . yet.

"Fuck it, we'll all go," said Luther.

"Do we need someone to stay in the car? I mean just in case," I said.

All three of them turned and looked at me.

"Okay, I'm in."

9

WE GOT OUT OF the SUV and headed for the place. "You know, I wouldn't mind right now if you did have the gun with you," I said.

"I've got it," Maggie said, and lifted her shirt in the back to show that it was shoved in the waist of her shorts.

"You're gonna shoot your ass off," said Russell.

"I could put it back in the car," she said.

"That's quite all right," said Luther. "No need for that."

The house was isolated by the large corner lot it sat on. A soft breeze moved the leaves of surrounding oaks, and if not for the fact that my heart was pounding, it would have been a perfect afternoon for a nap. The place gave no signs of life. Not the merest spark of light shone in any window, not the slightest ripple in any curtain. I thought of a line from *The Rime of the Ancient Mariner,* "As idle as a painted ship / Upon a painted ocean."

We walked in single file along the slate stone path from the street. Up on the porch our every step registered a creak in the splintered wood. Maggie knocked on the front door. While she waited for an answer, she stood with her hands behind her back, facing the floor. My mouth was dry. I was expecting something to suddenly tear the door open and pounce. Instead there was nothing. She pounded again, waited again, and then pounded another time.

"Try the knob," said Russell.

She did. It turned, and my heart sank. Luther looked at me and shook his head as Maggie and Russ opened the door and slipped inside. I checked behind us. No one in any of the houses even remotely close by could see what was going on, and you had to figure no one gave a shit either. I held the door for Luther, and the two of us followed.

Dim silence. It looked like an antiques shop and smelled like my grandmother in her latter, danker days. The front foyer opened onto a hallway, and we walked halfway down it before Maggie stopped Russell and yelled, "Hello?" The sound of her voice scared the crap out of me, and my body jerked.

"What the fuck?" I whispered.

Russ yelled, "Anybody home?"

I wanted to mention that we were going to get arrested when Luther elbowed me and said, "Check out this cat." He was pointing to an old photograph on the wall. It was of a gentleman in a long coat and hat. A thick brow, a hunched stature, like a caveman on a Henry James outing. I knew instantly it was Prewitt.

"Do you know who that is?" I asked Luther.

He shook his head.

"That's the guy who I think threw the baby in the privy."

"No way," he said, and moved closer to the photo and studied it.

By then, Maggie and Russell had each yelled three or four times. We were still in the hallway, waiting as if for the house itself to respond. It became clear that the walls there were lined with old photos and they seemed to be closing in on me. We quietly waited, and the spring tightened until Russell finally began to move forward.

"Do you think someone lives here?" asked Maggie.

"Yeah, that old lady you and Henry saw."

"Could have been a ghost," she said.

"Find the kitchen," said Luther. "Check the fridge if there is one and see if there's recent food in it."

It sounded way too logical to me. I wasn't happy about moving deeper into the heart of the old house. Dust bunnies scurried out of our path and much of the flowered upholstery was covered in a thin film of gray. We passed through a dining room, full place settings for each of the six chairs at the table. A grandfather clock stood in the corner and a grimy chandelier hung at the center of the ceiling. The floorboards complained at every step. I smelled smoke and noticed Maggie had lit up. If I'd had a joint, I'd have done the same.

The kitchen floor was a green-and-white checkerboard. On one side, there were the old appliances—refrigerator, stove, sink. And on the other side of the large room stood a table beneath an open window. Through it I could barely see the SUV parked up the block. Luther broke from the group and went to the refrigerator. It had the name Philco on it in chrome letters. When he opened the door, a light went on inside and illuminated a half head of lettuce, a container of milk, eggs, and other foods. He lifted the milk, screwed off the cap, and put the spout to his nose.

"Fresh," he said.

"I can't tell you how disappointing that is," I said.

Maggie took a couple more drags on her cig and then put it out under the faucet of the sink. "Let's go upstairs and see if we can find someone," she whispered.

To get to the stairs we had to backtrack through the dining room. My ears were doing that thing where you're listening so hard they twitch. There were goose bumps all down my neck and back. We passed through a living room, or what I suppose would have been a parlor in the mid-1920s. Russell pointed the beam from the flashlight app on his phone at the mantel of the fireplace, where there stood, next to an antique clock that still quietly

ticked, an old Nepenthe bottle holding a single mummi-
fied flower.

Beyond the living room, we found the stairs. I noticed
Russell had stepped aside and let Maggie take the lead. I
couldn't blame him. She reached behind and grabbed the
gun from her waistband. Up we went in single file. The
only spot worse than first was last, and somehow Luther
managed to get in front of me. If anyone in the house
didn't hear us ascending they'd have had to have been
deaf. The harder I tried to tiptoe, the worse the com-
plaints from the weary steps. We sounded like a herd of
something.

It was dark on the second floor, almost like early
evening. There were windows at either end of a long hallway, but they were covered in thick floor-length drapes.
Russell and Maggie put on their flashlight apps and we
proceeded to the first door across from the top of the
stairs. She pushed the door open and stepped inside with
the gun out in front of her. The three of us guys stood
behind and looked in over her shoulder. The room had a
four-poster bed, a dresser, a vanity, and a chair. The place
was in perfect order. It looked like there hadn't been anyone in that room in years.

Maggie began to back out, and I whispered, "Don't
you want to check the closet?"

"Go ahead," she said. Suffice it to say, I didn't. We

moved on to the next room on the right side of the hall-way heading toward the front of the house. Behind that closed door, we found a study that spread out larger than the previous bedroom. The flashlights revealed book-lined shelves, a desk with a globe on it, and a leather-backed reading chair. I wondered how many rare volumes sat on the shelves. I'd have loved to have had time to peruse the place with the drapes open. Maggie's light suddenly went out. "Shit," she said. "I'm out of juice."

Russell still had his light going, but he was across the room, exploring the darker back corner of it. My eyes were following him, as it was really the only light, save for what little came though the half-closed door behind us. It happened so quickly, I didn't have time to react. A pale figure stepped out of the thick shadows. Russell grunted in surprise. It was the old woman. Her thin, stringy hair was down around her shoulders, and the million wrin-kles of her face bobbed like there was nothing but water beneath them. I could barely make out her expression. Her eyes were wide with what could only be fear. Russ stepped back, and she stumbled forward to lean momen-tarily against his chest. Maggie lifted the gun and aimed.

In the distance of downstairs, I heard a door creak open and slam shut. The ancient woman gave a forced whisper. "Take this and get out!" she said. "It's coming. Run!" We were all stunned except for Luther, who raised his phone and had the wherewithal to snap a photo. Then we heard the thing on the stairs, taking one pounding step after another. It sounded like it was halfway to the second floor already. I had seen Maggie's flashlight beam, before it died, sweep over a closet door. I lunged in that direction, tripped over a stack of books that had been left on the floor, managed to stay on my feet, and reached the door in about two seconds. I opened it and slipped inside.

Luckily there was enough room in that closet for me to fit, with some extra besides. I surmised it was a walk-in. I stood in the dark, my arms wrapped around myself as if I were cold, though I was sweating, and tried to control my breathing. I nearly pissed when the door shot open. I expected the Pariah, but it was Russell, looking for a place to hide. "Hurry," I said so softly even I could hardly hear myself. I shut the door behind him and we stood, listening. No more than a moment later, we heard the door to the study sweep back and bang against the wall.

The flashlight was still lit on Russell's phone. I pointed to it and held my phone up, trying to indicate I was going to text him. I remembered to turn the sound all the way down before I started typing. I asked him what happened to Maggie and Luther. I watched as he wrote back to me. "Maggie is under the desk and Luther, I think, got out of the room." Since we hadn't heard any screams as of then,

I figured everybody was okay.

"What about the old woman?" I wrote.

"Not sure. She gave me something."

Then we heard the Pariah snarl, and Russ and I killed the phones. The phantom/creature was moving around the study. I heard the old woman moaning. The Pariah let out a loud growl, followed by the sound of books hitting the floor. The thing was working itself up into a rage. It began snuffling, sniffing around for prey it knew was somewhere nearby. More things were toppled, and the old woman was sobbing.

Everything went quiet, and I wondered if the Pariah and the woman had left the study. I put my hand on Russell's forearm to get his attention. Turning my phone on, I motioned that I was going to open the door a crack to see what was up. He nodded. The moment I'd volunteered, I regretted it. I reached out, put my hand on the doorknob, and froze. We stood there for a few seconds, and he leaned over and whispered in my ear, "Come on."

The door flew open, but not under my power. Russell held up his lit phone and we saw the swirling smoke of the spirit coalesce before the opening to the closet. In the blink of an eye, that smoke became a solid figure, like water instantly becoming ice. The face was catlike, doglike, vicious, and saliva flew off its lips. As it opened wide its snout, Russell punched it as hard as he could with his free ham fist and lunged forward like in a blocking drill. He budged the creature backward and bounded for the door to the study. I was right behind him. The lights came on, and I couldn't follow everything after that.

All I knew was that it was Maggie at the light switch by the door. As I passed her, she lifted the gun and pulled the trigger. The blast from it deafened me, but I kept running. Russ was ahead of me, and I could feel the gun barrel in my back shoving me along down the stairs. When we reached the bottom, I turned and looked and saw the whipping, twirling storm cloud of the Pariah descending after us. That was it; I didn't look back again but ran through the house, out the front door, down the steps, and straight to the SUV.

I was relieved to see Luther there already, holding the back door open for me. Russell was in the driver's seat starting it up, and Maggie was climbing into the passenger seat. We pulled away from that curb like we were pulling out of the pit at Daytona. Eventually, three blocks later, Maggie punched Russell in the shoulder to get his attention and said, "Slow down." He did, and we cruised along all jittery.

Luther was the first to speak. "What the fucking fuck?" he said.

"This is getting too crazy for me." I could hear my voice trembling.

Russell turned to Maggie and asked, "What happened when you shot it?"

Maggie lit a cig and opened her window. "The bullet passed through it and sort of pulled the rest of the monster into the bullet hole and it disappeared. Does that make sense?"

Russell shook his head. "That doesn't make any sense," he said.

"I know," she said. "It was like something you'd see in a cartoon. And that poor old lady. Jeez, what the fuck's happening with her?"

"I got the feeling she was trapped there," said Luther. "I thought at first she was a ghost."

"She gave me something," said Russell. He took the wheel with one hand and dug into his pocket with the other. "Maybe a note." Keeping his eyes on the road, he handed the ripped scrap of yellow paper to Maggie. "Is there a message on it?"

The paper was folded in half. Maggie opened it and nodded. "'The Demon Mind.'"

Luther and I both laughed. Maggie turned back and looked over the seat at us. "What's wrong with you two? This thing's killing people."

"I know," I said. "It's . . ."

"It's ridiculous," said Russell.

I had them drop me off at home. It was getting on twilight and I definitely didn't want to play anymore. I was worried that thing might come for my father in retaliation for us breaking into the old lady's house. I made him a good dinner and stuck close to him, watching two old horror movies back to back. I asked him not to go walking, and to my surprise, he went along with me. The only time I spent out of the tobacco den was to use the bathroom, and later, once he'd gone to sleep in the chair, to smoke a joint out on the front porch. I couldn't even enjoy that, though. All I could think was, *Say the Pariah sneaks in and rips him up while I'm partying?*

When I went back inside, I turned off the TV and sat in the quiet. I knew there was an email on my phone from Maggie. It had come through an hour and a half earlier, but the thought of opening it scared me. I leaned back against the arm of the couch, slipped my sneaks off, and curled my legs up. I was weary beyond reckoning. I held the phone in my hand and closed my eyes. Immediately, I could feel the current of sleep pulling me downriver.

At the last second, I couldn't let myself go. I gave in and opened the damn email.

10

MAGGIE MUST HAVE BEEN cooking on three Sudafed and a big cup of coffee, because her writing was frenetic and full of errors. I could see that she'd cc'd Russell and Luther and Joe as well, and I wondered if they had taken the bait. She wrote that once she'd gotten back to her house, she got on the computer and started researching the phrase "The Demon Mind." If she'd had to search for "The Mind of a Demon," there would have been a million-plus hits. As it turned out, what she searched only brought up seven thousand. "And then to narrow it down," she said.

She coupled the phrase in quotes with some name or thing from our investigations into the demon baby. Like "The Demon Mind" and "Prewitt." "There was so much crap to dig through," she said. "Bad horror book titles and cards from kids' fantasy games, etc." She went through all the qualifying terms she could think of. "Marlby" "1923" "Arbenville" "Twilight Pariah" "Humboldt." She scanned through hundreds of pages with the find function, but came up with nothing. When she was getting fed up, she remembered the Kind Nepenthe and fed that into the Web with the phrase "The Demon Mind." Nothing.

Eventually, she gave up and went out by the pool bar to have a drink, and when she poured a tumbler of rum, she thought of Kind Nepenthe again, but this time with the name of its inventor, Anchill. She went back to the computer and fed those two search terms in, and bingo. Dr. Richard Anchill had published a book in 1933, *The Demon Mind*. "And get this," she wrote. "Someone transcribed that tome for the Internet and posted it on Project Gutenberg. I couldn't fuckin' believe it. I should have dug deeper when I initially looked him up.

"I'm sure this is the document the old woman who slipped Russ the note wanted us to find. It's a chapter from this book about pharmaceutical treatments Anchill used in his practice as a therapist. It's attached. Read it. Call me in the morning." As tired as I was, I read it. It wasn't a link to the pages on Project Gutenberg but instead she'd cut and pasted it into her email.

And now, dear reader, we come to what was without doubt the strangest case of my long career. I, like many of my colleagues who graduated with degrees in the mind sciences during the early 1890s had by 1915, after the publication of John B. Watson's seminal work, pushed the analysis-based treatment of Freud aside and turned wholeheartedly toward behaviorism. For a profession that was often held in ridicule and suspected of having, like the emperor, no clothes, the scientific approach based not in dreams and whimsy but in that which is objectifiable and evident to anyone with eyes and ears seemed a great boon to the pursuit. It seemed to make perfect sense to me—that is, until I met the young woman who I will be discussing in this chapter. After she became my patient, Science itself became increasingly more suspect.

I will refer to her as M. to protect her identity. She came to me on a winter's afternoon in a state of great agitation. Her family was well-off and could afford my services, but her case was so interesting, I think I would have taken it on pro bono. When she was first ushered into my office by her mother, she was trembling, which I thought was a reaction to the biting cold of that January. I had my wife make us tea, and we sat before the fire, the warmth of which did nothing to quell her shaking. When I asked the mother what the problem seemed to be, she told me her daughter was haunted.

"I see," I said, and wrote that down in my notes. The girl was pretty, with short brown hair, green eyes, and a distinctive birthmark on her left cheek that did not subtract from her looks but accentuated them. Besides being upset, she seemed otherwise a healthy young woman of thirteen. I inquired as to when the problem began, and the mother said, "A month or two ago." But the girl shook her head most violently and said, "No, three years ago, on the Fourth of July."

"Please explain," I said.

She took a deep breath and worked for a moment to calm herself. "Mother and Father and I were at the celebration downtown and it was almost night. I'd left their side and went looking for some of my friends from school. I'd had two lemonades and had to urinate, but there was nowhere to go, so I crawled into some bushes near the post office." The girl's mother was aghast and admonished M. roundly for using the word "urinate" and for having crawled into the bushes to do so.

"Ma'am," I said, "it's perfectly fine. Your daughter used the appropriate word, and it's hard to find a crime in her actions." M. looked at me and I saw a slight smile, as if she was beginning to perceive in me an ally. "Carry on, dear."

"I was hiding in the bushes. No one was around. I'd finished what I'd gone in there for, but as I was about to crawl out, I noticed someone approaching. It was a man with a strange-looking dog on a leash. I didn't want him to see me crawling out, so I stayed put and waited for them to pass. Then the leash got tangled in the dog's back legs and the man yelled at the dog. The dog cowered and made a sad face with big eyes like a baby about to cry. The dog could see me where I hid and looked at me for help. The man beat him and cursed him and . . . it was terrible. It was . . ." The girl fell silent and stared into the crackling fire.

I tried a different approach to get to the crux of the story. "And what kind of dog was it?" I asked.

M. remained silent and I could tell she was reliving the incident. There were tears forming in her eyes and they glistened in the reflection of the firelight. The mother was repeating, "Terrible, terrible," in a low whisper, like a penitent in church saying the rosary. The girl finally shook her head as if waking from a dream and said, "An ugly dog with a pushed-in snout and a wrinkled forehead, short brown-and-black fur. Anyone would say the dog was ugly, but I felt bad for her. He beat her and beat her and the dog whimpered and I could tell she didn't understand."

"People can be so cruel," I said. "But how exactly did that contribute to the problem you've come to speak to me about today?"

"Well," said M. "The memory of that poor dog stayed in my head. At first it was a small bump in my thoughts, like a seed beneath my memory. A while later it started to grow and I could feel it growing. I kept going back to it and touching it with my memory like when you have a loose tooth and you touch it with your tongue. I couldn't forget it. I kept seeing it over and again and the poor sad face of that dog huddled down, not understanding."

"I see. And does it keep you up at night and give you bad dreams?"

"Over the past summer, it did," said her mother.

I nodded.

"But then it grew so much," said M., "that it grew into something else."

"Interesting," I said, and wrote away in my casebook. "What did it grow into?"

"It grew into a baby with horns and claws and a pointed tale. A bumpy back like a dragon. Its eyes were like cat eyes. It looked scary, but it was afraid, I could tell. I comforted it and sang songs to it in my head." The mother looked at me from behind her daughter and raised her eyebrows, slightly shook her head. "It lived in my thoughts, in my ideas," the girl added.

"Fascinating," I said. "And so should I assume that you wish for me to help you be rid of it?"

The girl stared at me. "You can't."

I continued to see M. in a professional manner even after I had dropped my other patients in lieu of working in the pharmaceutical field for Hespera, Merck's main competitor at the time. Her "condition" not only remained but evolved into something stranger. As it did, she became more adept at discussing it and its effects upon her. I applied my behaviorist theories in an attempt to get her to change her lifestyle. My hope was to alter her situation in hopes of altering the state of her mind. If anything, she became more obsessed with the entity that had sprung up from that witnessed incident of brutality.

When she was seventeen, she came to see me one day without her mother. We didn't have an appointment, and she caught me just before I was leaving for work early in the morning. I had a meeting at the office that morning and almost dismissed her, telling her to come back that evening, but she said she'd snuck out of the house and ridden her bicycle to my place two towns away as to be able to see me without her mother present. She looked very agitated; her face was flushed and she was taking rapid breaths. It could have been from her riding, but she'd sat for an hour after my wife had let her in while I was dressing.

We went into my home office by the fire, and no sooner had we sat down than she said, "Watch this, Doctor." I nodded. A few moments later I noticed a kind of vague smoke appeared to be emanating from the crown of her head. I reached for the pitcher of water on the table beside us, believing beyond reason that somehow her hair had caught fire. She put a hand upon my arm to stay me. I sat transfixed, watching the swirling smoke rise up into a pillar five feet tall above her.

"Now," M. said to me, and the column of smoke left her and floated down to the floor. I was in awe. The thing seemed to be changing and I saw in it the outline of a young woman, like a silhouette thrown by a lantern in fog. The clarity of the figure focused and blurred intermittently, and I never got a clear view. When it moved, the tendrils of smoke swirled around it and roiled like storm clouds within its general form. It moved slowly about the room and then headed back toward us. My mind was blank with wonder, all my scientific certainties sundered in a matter of seconds. I grasped on to the thought that it was no doubt a parlor trick.

When it had returned to M.'s side, it suddenly lunged at me and in an instant coalesced into a physical creature with fangs and horns and demon eyes. It growled and barked, and I pushed back in my chair and literally screamed. Next I knew, it had vanished and a light gray residue drifted toward the floor, quickly evaporating as it fell. You can imagine my state of mind. The young woman was smiling.

"You're the first person I've revealed it to," she said.

I poured a glass of water and drank it down, got up from my chair, and made a circuit of the room, swinging my arms and breathing deeply. After collecting my wits, I sat again and inquired, "And what exactly is it?" I asked.

"It's part of me," she said. "I grew it."

"Is it a spirit that's possessed you?"

"No, it's part of me."

"Can you control it?"

"No. But I watch it and see what it does. It's not brain smart, but it has very deep and strong emotions."

"I should say. There seemed to be two forms to it. One, if you don't mind my saying, looked like it could have been you if you were made of thick fog. The other was some kind of animal."

M. nodded. "It comes and goes from me, but we are always attached. If I care to, I can see what it sees. It travels out of me, almost invisibly into the world, sometimes as smoke, sometimes as just a dullness in an otherwise sunny day. It can only become real or have a body for a short time, and when it does that takes a lot of energy from me."

"Does it have an intention? Is it trying to destroy you or take you over?"

"No. It protects me. You see, it's worried about you, so that's why it tried to scare you just now."

"Well, it was quite successful, I must say."

"It lives with me, in my head, like my mind is an apartment. I think it's something that grew from my imagination. Please, don't tell my mother. I've been able to avoid having her find out. She'd be too frightened for me."

I nodded. "I'll keep it quiet for now. Come back and see me Saturday, but come alone on your bicycle."

She nodded and stood up. "Thank you so much, Dr. Anchill."

"Yes," I said, and smiled to reassure her, although I probably needed more reassurance than she. "Tell me one other thing. Is it still connected to you when you sleep? I mean, does it roam your dreams?"

"Then it has most control. It shows me things, beautiful places and creatures. It has wings in my dreams and flies me into the treetops and mountain peaks."

Yes, dear reader, what was I to think? I wasn't completely convinced that this was not some form of trickery. I was familiar with the charlatanry of table rappers, mentalists, fortune tellers, the psychic whim-wham of the Fox sisters. Houdini himself had debunked all of this. The one thing a spiritualist fraud needs to be successful (and there is money to be made in bilking the naive) is to enchant a professional like myself. I was suspicious, but at the same time, M. seemed so genuine, so innocent, devoid of guile. I decided to bolster myself against jumping to conclusions and instead to calm my racing mind and take things methodically, rationally.

As it was, I dared not reveal the particulars of this case to my colleagues. My main reason was I didn't want to be laughed out of the profession, and my next was to keep it under wraps so I might have it to myself to investigate. Even the study of a charlatan could offer some interesting psychological perspectives. I continued to see M. in my home office, and I managed to convince her mother that she was doing fine and it would be no problem for her to visit me by herself. All of this was contingent upon the ability of the young woman to continue to hide the facts of her condition from her parents, which miraculously she managed.

In the years that followed, as she grew into adulthood, I, a man of science, came to the ready conclusion that what she had told me was every bit true. I made a slow and meticulous study of her "affliction (?)"—not that I learned much more than on that first day she revealed the existence of Petra, which is how she came to refer to the smoke entity. I call it an entity only out of the paucity of human language to describe the supernatural. Alas, one cannot name what one does not know. This was something far beyond reason. The universe had either erred or engaged in artistry but gave up no answers as to the how and why of it. All I really could count on is what she told me.

It was the summer of 1906; we met in the garden out behind my house. The day was beautifully clear and the blossoms were at their peak. It was then that she told me she was getting married and that she wanted me to help her separate from Petra. "Won't she know?" I asked.

"She's out of me now, but it wouldn't make a difference. She doesn't understand treachery."

"What would you have me do?" I asked. My initial reaction was a selfish one, and I wondered what would become of my research. But, in the long run, I took a deep breath and drew myself back to humanity. I promised her I would help her. I didn't tell her this at the time, but I had a spark of a thought that strangely had never struck before. My main work during those years was in pharmaceuticals. I wondered if a chemical cure was possible.

My thought was not to be so drastic as to try to cure her in one fell swoop, but instead to begin by giving her brief periods where Petra, once away from her, could not return until the medicine wore off. At least M. might have her mind to herself in those spans. Perhaps after, we could learn to extend them. I needed something that would quite seriously scramble her thought processes. I proceeded by believing whatever M. had told me. A dangerous course, I'll admit. With that as my guide, I aimed my initial attack at her consciousness.

The weapon I chose was one I'd recently been looking at in my pharmaceutical work. A seed from the flower known as the Devil's Trumpet. It's of the genus vespertine, poisonous plants that only blossom after dusk. It had several names—jimson weed, hell's bells, thorn apple, devil's weed. The Mayans called it "Datura." The effects that had been reported from the ingestion of the seeds were disorientation, delirium, an inability to distinguish between reality and fantasy. And a most important aspect of it was that it didn't put the subject to sleep but held them in a twilight state.

I created a concoction to give to M., boiling the active ingredients out of the seeds and mixing them with a blend of caffeine, good bourbon, and a hint of sweetness (a liberal addition of raw sugar, which made the potion wonderfully viscous). I administered it to her in my office on the Saturday before her wedding.

By that time, she'd come to the conviction that she must get rid of the entity and was eager to sample the concoction. We waited until Petra left her. Once the thing had vacated M.'s mind, I had her drink four ounces of the dark syrup. The Datura showed its effects rapidly, with a dilating of the pupils, a quickening of the heartbeat and breathing. Some minor perspiration. Those affects increased, though, and grew more wild as the drug took ahold of her. For a good fifteen minutes I had to stand over her and hold her forearms tightly against the chair arms in order to keep her in her seat. She mumbled incoherencies and shook as if freezing. I was worried I might have prescribed too much.

Eventually she calmed down and leaned back in the chair. She sat for nearly two hours, staring out my office window, somewhere between wakefulness and sleep. I felt as if she was at peace for the first time since developing the entity. And then Petra returned. The thing came in my open office door like a smoke tornado, heading directly for M. But it was brought up short by the jumbled inaccessibility of her thoughts. I heard the thing growl. It swept around my office, lifting papers into flight. It came together as a creature in instantaneous bursts, knocking books to the floor, overturning a chair by the window, appearing before me and pushing me over backward in my chair.

I scrambled to my feet and sidled away to the corner of the room. Luckily, M. began to come around by then. She groaned and shook her head. No doubt with the first shred of lucidity Petra found its way back in. After she'd recovered from the experience, I inquired as to the results. She was ecstatic about the ability to finally be alone for a while. She thanked me profusely and asked if we could repeat the treatment upon her next visit. Instead I told her I wanted her to administer it to herself once a day. I gave her four bottles of the Kind Nepenthe to take with her.

She continued with the treatment and told me that those hours of freedom from Petra made her life worthwhile. She'd married a very wealthy local man, and she'd explained to him her affliction and the need for her treatment. He wanted only for her to be well. I was concerned about the long-term effects of the drug upon her. Each time I saw her she looked more weary and drawn. I told her that I thought we should discontinue the treatments until she got her full health back. Only then did she tell me the truth. She was pregnant. Not only was she pregnant, but she said she knew that Petra was shaping her unborn child, infiltrating its skin and bone and blood, making a future home for itself in the world. She confessed to having increased the dosage of the Nepenthe (as I'd since come to call the medicine) from once a day to twice a day.

"I need more time with my child alone," she said. "I'm wrestling with Petra over the control of my baby."

11

I GOT A CALL from Maggie first thing the next morning, which was a Saturday. She told me that Sondra was being laid to rest over at the municipal cemetery later that morning at eleven thirty. It was nauseating for me to think about what had happened. Not because of any relationship we'd had, but the thought of how beautiful and vital and interesting a person she was, and let's not forget the fact that our meddling in the Prewitt history was largely responsible for her death. I didn't want to admit to that guilt. Maggie told me we had to face it, and so I agreed to be ready if she swung by with the Galaxie at eleven to get me.

The ceremony at the grave site was a somber affair and the poor girl's parents were distraught. The police chief was there looking sheepish since he had no leads and no suspects. I wished I could have spilled the whole crazy saga to him, but it would have been pointless. I came away from the ceremony with tears in my eyes and a real rage in my chest. I imagine Maggie felt the same, because once we got in her car to leave, she turned to me and said,

"Henry, we have to stop this thing."

I put my arm around her and drew her close. "I know," I said. "I'm ready."

"We need a plan," she said.

On the way to her place, she called Russell and asked if he and Luther could meet us there. Next, she quizzed me on Anchill's unfinished account. "What'd you think of it?" she asked.

"It's . . . wacko."

"I know, the thing growing from the memory of a mean dog owner beating its dog, to Anchill drugging her with that shit cocktail he whipped up, to the fact that Petra was forming the baby."

"Well, obviously, Petra won," I said.

"There's a lot in that account for us to go on, though, Henry. I went through the piece at least five times and made notes."

"What are we gonna do, suck it into a bottle like the genie in Aladdin?"

"Do you have that Xerox pic of Marlby Prewitt?"

"Actually, I haven't washed these jeans in about two weeks. It's still folded up in my back pocket."

"The clothes make the man."

We convened by the pool. Russell and Luther told us they'd stayed away from the funeral that morning to avoid suspicion by the police. Russ had already been questioned in the Kerbb killings; he didn't want to be a potential suspect in this one as well.

I made a pitcher of whiskey sours and served them each with a trio of maraschino cherries. There was a lot of wincing at the tartness of the cocktails, but nobody abandoned theirs. And the one pitcher became two. When we were all loose, Maggie said, "We've got to destroy this thing before it kills again."

Luther said, "Yeah," and Russell and I nodded.

Maggie asked Luther about the photo he'd taken of the old woman when we'd snuck into the house. He lifted his phone out of his shirt pocket and checked for it. "You know, I haven't even looked at it myself yet," he said. "Too weirded out still."

Maggie asked me for the copier portrait of Marlby. I gave it to her and she shook her head as she unfolded it, flattening it out on the bar. She grabbed Luther's phone and brought it before her so she could see both images at once. "Look," she said, pointing with her free hand. "The birthmark. It's the same. After reading Anchill's case history last night and with this to corroborate it, I'm willing to say I think this woman is Marlby Prewitt. Anybody disagree?"

She looked over at Russell, who was obviously unhappy agreeing with anything about the Twilight Pariah, but he must have come to the only rational conclusion, namely that Marlby Prewitt was still alive, because he said nothing. Maggie upped the ante and told us that she believed that the entity, as Anchill called it, was somehow keeping the old lady alive past the normal bounds of mortality. "She's been in the clutches of that thing for over a hundred years."

"The thought of that just raised the hair on my forearms," said Luther.

"Okay, so what do we do?" asked Russell.

"We wait a few minutes," said Maggie, and checked her watch.

"Why are we waiting?"

"For the last member of our group. Everyone has to be here when we make the plan."

"You mean Crazy College?" said Russell.

"Yeah, Joe Medley," she said.

"Did you give Russ his bag of lawn clippings and Luther his bag of salt?" I asked.

"Not yet."

"What's that?" asked Luther.

I described our last meeting at the diner with the professor. Even Maggie laughed, and she was still laughing when lo and behold Joe Medley appeared at her side gate and let himself into the yard. Immediately he inquired as to what we'd been laughing about when he entered. I told him I was telling Russell about the other night at the diner when he gave out the weapon bags.

He straightened the clasp of his string tie and said, "More in heaven and earth," nodded, and smiled. I poured him a whiskey sour and Luther asked if any of us had read the preface to *The Demon Mind*.

"If you read the preface it says that the book was published posthumously and that Anchill had died under mysterious circumstances. It never could be conclusively determined if he'd been murdered or taken down by a wild animal."

"Hoist with his own petard," I said.

"Petra must have sensed that the doctor was behind all those hours she was severed from M.," said Luther. "I have a feeling that the entity's rage is a result of a sense of betrayal. It explodes after building for years, and then people die."

"Here's what I've got in mind," said Maggie, "based on the book chapter and what we've learned so far. In *The Demon Mind*, Anchill states that the Kind Nepenthe temporarily cut the psychic cord between M. and Petra. There ensued a window of almost two hours where Marlby Prewitt's mind was her own. Petra was shut out. If anything happened in that time, it could not flee back to M.'s thoughts. That's when the thing is most vulnerable, and that's when I think we should kill it."

There was silence for a while, and then Russell said,

"That plan makes some monumental assumptions. I mean, to make this work we'd have to drug Gang of Wrinkles with around four ounces of Kind Nepenthe, which means we'd have to have four ounces and we'd have to administer it to her ourselves."

"Even if we're able to do that, we've got to kill it, which seems easier said than done. You can't even shoot the fucking thing. It just disappears and comes back later," I said.

"We've got to get it in those few seconds when it comes together in a physical form. Then we can attack it."

"There's nothing that's gonna kill it."

"Henry, remember your father told us that story about drinking at the Prewitt place and getting chased by the ghost? You remember how the thing shrieked and vanished?"

"Wait a second, you're risking our lives against a supernatural monster based on what my old man told you?"

She nodded. "Fire." She recounted my father's story for the others.

"I can't tell you what bad odds that story has of being true," I said.

"I believe him," said Maggie.

"Fire is as good a suggestion as anything else," said Russell. "We know bullets don't work."

"Then how do we get it to coalesce when we need it to

in order to attack it?" I asked.

"The baby skeleton. That's what I think it's after. It knows we have it, and I think that's why it hasn't killed us yet. Afraid if it kills us, it'll never see the child again. We lure it in with that, and when it materializes to take the skeleton, we douse it with gasoline and set it and the whole Prewitt place on fire."

"Wow," said Luther. "The whole place?"

"So we can be sure we got it," she said.

"And my last question," I said. Before I could continue, though, the professor stepped forward and took a small, thin paper packet from his inside jacket pocket. He flipped back the top flap and poured its contents onto the bar. "Datura seed," he said. He knew I was going to ask about the Nepenthe. "We'll make our own. The ingredients are clear enough in Anchill's book."

Luther asked him where he had gotten the seeds.

"Devil's Trumpet grows wild in my garden. I can't get rid of it."

"Whatever you do, don't let Russell pick the bourbon for the recipe," I said.

The professor oversaw the brewing of the Kind Nepenthe in Maggie's kitchen. The AC was on high, but still Medley sweated like an Easter pig. He stood over a boiling pot and called for the ingredients. When we went to the liquor store to get the bourbon, Luther had the idea that we should use 5-hour ENERGY shots instead of coffee, which was what the professor had originally intended to use.

"The Kind Nepenthe smells pretty unkind," said Maggie.

"If this shit doesn't cure her it'll kill her," said Russell.

"Yeah, what happens when and if the thing succumbs to the fire and it dies? Does that mean she's gonna die too? Does her real age instantly catch up to her like in a Poe story and she's transformed into a pool of black putrescence?"

"Henry, you ask more questions than a fucking five-year-old," said Maggie. "Shut up and hand me that cleaned-out Nepenthe bottle." We gathered around as she ladled up a steeping draught and poured it into the pint bottle over the sink. Steam rose as we watched the aquamarine glass go dark with the rising elixir. When it was full, Maggie stuffed a cork from a bottle of wine we'd finished off that afternoon into the end of it. "To Marlby Prewitt," she said, and held the Nepenthe high. Me and Russell and Luther applauded. Joe Medley took out one of his red rolled joints and lit up in celebration. This time, he passed it.

We were ready to take on the dreaded Twilight Pariah with our bottle of brown punch and tiny sacks of salt and rice. The sun was on the descent, and we all sat out by the pool, waiting. Since I wasn't driving that night, I had a few more to quell my nerves. I wasn't completely convinced we were doing the right thing, and the plan was so wacky, what with the red rolled weed, I never could think of all the steps at once. Maggie volunteered to be the one to go to Marlby Prewitt's place and coax the old lady to drink, and the other four of us would go together in Russell's SUV out to the mansion and set things up.

"Don't forget," said Maggie. "When I call you on the phone, I'll be on my way to you to help, but that will be the alert that Petra is separated from Marlby's mind."

We all nodded, but none of us, I was sure, knew what we were approving of. Finally, the time came. The sky was pink in the west and there were less than twenty minutes to sundown. We carefully unloaded the skeleton from Maggie's trunk and put it on the blue blanket surrounded by full cans of gasoline in the way-back part of Russell's SUV. I couldn't help but think the little bugger was smiling at us.

I reminded Maggie to pack her gun and she ran from the driveway back to the pool to get her shoulder bag. When she returned, I gave her a hug and she went around and hugged everyone, even creepy old Joe, who seemed to hold on for an extra heartbeat. When we got into the SUV, Russell and Luther sat up front and it was me and the professor in the back. "I'll partner with

Luther," said Russ, "and Joe, you and Henry are a team." The big man looked into the rearview mirror and smirked at me. Joe didn't notice; he was handing out bags of rice and salt.

As we rode toward the mansion, Luther said, "Maggie's got to be one of the daringest people I've ever met. She's gonna break in on a 127-year-old woman and convince her to take a big drink of brown stuff. What if the Pariah doesn't go out this twilight?" It was so unthinkable that none of us bothered to answer. Luther didn't even expect us to. As we drove out of town into the gathering dark, my heart began to pound. The professor was farting to beat the band.

We arrived in the dark, and Russell took the lantern out of his car and gave me the good flashlight. Joe had his own, as did Luther. We each took a can of gasoline and poured it around on different floors of the house but saved a liberal amount to fill a glass jar and to douse the armoire in the basement. That hulking piece of furniture was to be the epicenter of our attack. The baby skeleton was to stay in the car until we heard from Maggie. Once everything was prepared the way she'd instructed us, we sat in twos at either end of the basement, north and south, and waited.

I wasn't exactly sure how to make small talk with the professor, but I tried, as it was too creepy just sitting there on a broken-down divan without legs in the black silence. "You read the account," I said. "Do you know of any other example of a creature growing from the mind of a man or woman?"

"I'm put in mind of the tulpas of Tibet, what the Buddhist adepts call a 'thought-form creation.' A being concocted from sheer mind power. The explorer Alexandra David-Neel attested that she'd studied the techniques of tulpa creation while in Tibet. She said she created a thought-form companion based on Falstaff, who eventually became a solid, physical human being. This fellow accompanied her on her journeys until she sensed he was trying to sabotage her, and then she had to have him killed."

"That's true?"

"Look it up, my friend. More in heaven and earth. There is also the discovery of what is called 'a unilaterally felt presence,' when a certain section of the brain, the temporoparietal junction, is affected, damaged, or stimulated. One most convincingly detects another person standing nearby. So, yes, there are instances in the literature, but trust me, there's nothing like this. And that's the difficulty." Joe Medley reached into the pocket of his too-large suit jacket, pulled out yet another joint, and lit it.

"What's the difficulty?"

"What we're up against here is by all accounts impossible, yet it obviously is happening. We have dead bodies to prove it. But it can't be easily stopped, because those we need to convince about its existence—for instance, the police—won't believe it, not having experienced it." He passed the joint to me, and I knew it was a bad idea, but I took a hit out of nervousness. Before I knew it, the thing was smoked and I was blazed.

"What strikes me about this whole thing," I said, "is, think of how the cruelty of that dog owner has echoed through time to affect the present. That bad karma radiated out to infect everything around it."

"Well put, sir," said Joe, and lightly tamped his failing hair as if to make sure he was ready for his close-up.

12

WE'D SAT THERE IN the dark talking bullshit for like an hour when my phone rang. With the sudden noise, my ass lifted a foot off the broken-down divan. I answered. "How are you two doing over that way?" asked Russell.

"So far, so scared," I said.

"Us too. Luckily, I have Luther. Hey, we're seeing a light shining somewhere behind where you guys are."

I stood up and turned around. A fairly bright source shone off to the west, somewhere out in the wilds of the cellar.

"What is it?"

"How am I supposed to know?" I said.

"You want to go check it out?"

"Are you kidding?"

"It could be important," said Russell. "You really should go. . . ."

"Okay, okay, okay, I'm going," I said.

"Don't forget to have your bag of rice handy."

I asked if he'd heard from Maggie yet, but he'd already hung up.

The professor said he would accompany me, and we slowly headed off in the direction of the light. Having smoked now made me twice as paranoid. Medley didn't seem to be very excited at all. He shuffled along through the dark like a zombie. We moved around the old columns and amid the debris littering the floor. A rat crossed our path at one point and I yelped, only to have Joe quietly shush me with his boney finger to his lips.

The light we came upon was very bright and encompassed a ten-yard circle in its glow. When we finally got close enough to determine what was creating the beacon, a chill shot up my spine. I called Russell. He answered. "That light? It's one of the fucking lanterns the thing stole from us."

"Shit," said Russ. "That means it's here, and it knows we're here."

"What do we do?"

"Maggie just called me before you. She's on her way. She said she got the old woman to drink the Nepenthe. Luther's getting the skeleton out of the car. Meet us at the armoire. And bring the lantern so we have plenty of light." He hung up.

I hesitated for a moment, unable to focus on what we were up to. Finally, I shook my head, grabbed up the lantern, and said, "We've got to hurry. Stick with me." I wasn't running but walking awfully fast. Medley, on the other hand, was slow-motion running on his tiptoes. It was ridiculous. He wasn't any faster that way than in his usual somnambulist lurching. The lantern was a godsend, though, as we could see a large swath ahead of us instead of a simple beam's worth. We made it to the armoire only to find that Luther and Russell had beat us there.

They had the mirrored doors on the old piece of furniture open and Luther was carefully placing the baby inside the compartment that he and I had initially discovered Petra in. When he backed away, we saw that he'd positioned the skeleton sitting, leaning against the inner wall, with its elbow resting on its knee and its finger bones fixed so that it was baring the middle digit at us.

I had to laugh; so did Russell, who stepped over to Luther, pulled him in for a hug, and kissed him.

"You're crazy," he said.

"A sense of levity is all to the better," said the professor, still slightly out of breath from his jog.

I watched as Russell pulled the jar of gasoline from his sweatshirt pocket. "So when it reaches for the baby, I'm gonna douse it. Who's got a lighter?"

Joe and I both acknowledged that we did.

"What we need is a cigarette," said Luther. "With only a lighter, you're going to have to get pretty damn close to the thing to light the gas on fire."

"I never thought of that. Maybe Maggie will get here

before the shit hits the fan."

Russell took out a length of macramé cord he'd gotten at Maggie's. He tied it to the doorknob on the armoire and then closed the doors. It was his conjecture that if we made a sudden reveal of the skeleton, the entity would be caught off guard. As soon as he finished knotting it, a sound came from directly behind us. We all spun around. Maggie stepped out of the dark and said, "What a scene with Marlby Prewitt. I'll tell you later."

"We haven't laid eyes on it yet, but we know it's here," said Russell.

"Oh, I just saw it up in the living room. I ran past it to get to the stairs. It's on its way."

"It's coming, now?" I said.

"Give me a cigarette," said Luther. She did and he lit it. But the smoke seemed to gather around his head too quickly, and we realized Petra was among us. I froze solid, too paralyzed to move. It materialized and lashed out at me, slicing my cheek and chest. The pain of these wounds instantly throbbed. I lay there for a moment and then somehow sat up. I saw the entity weave its way around Russell, and in the instant it coalesced, it raked its claws across his back. It punched Maggie in the face and then headed back for me. I could tell by the fire in its eyes that it meant to devour me.

I'm not exactly sure what happened, but somewhere

in the action the professor appeared beside me. As the smoke began to transform into flesh in front of us, he reached into his jacket pocket and retrieved a small plastic pouch. The fangs and claws took on existence, and he turned the bag upside down and emptied the contents at his feet. The Pariah lunged, and in mid-pounce stopped, fell to its knees, and moaned. It swept the rice up in only three passes, which was just enough time for Medley to help me to my feet and away from it.

I backed out of the glow of the lantern that had fallen from my hand and watched. The smoke was whirling crazily around the others. It turned in an instant to muscle and flesh and bone and pounced on Russell. Catching its paws close to his face, he kneed it in the midsection. It exploded into smoke. He searched the ground and in a few seconds found the end of the cord. He pulled it, the cord came loose, and the other end fell on the ground. "Fuck," he said, and reached for his bag of salt. Out of the dark, the thing was on him. He doused it with salt, but it wasn't the salt that prevented him from being slaughtered. Luther had crawled to the armoire door and pulled it open.

The smoke slowly took the form of a woman. It moved its tentacle arms out toward the armoire, fingertips and face continually forming and dissolving into fog. I knew what had to happen now, and it had to happen quickly.

Russell unscrewed the jar of gasoline. Maggie, despite having just been punched in the face, still had her cigarette going. They moved in behind the entity as it drifted toward the armoire. From where I stood, I could see in the lantern light, through shifting mists, the skeleton of the baby in the armoire. The entity made a sickening, mournful noise.

I saw it come together with horns and snapping tail, and I saw it lean into the armoire and gather the child's remains in its arms. It made a sound like a long sigh, and Joe Medley called out from behind me in his loudest whisper, "Now."

Russell tossed the gas and drenched it. There was the splash, but before Maggie could flick her cigarette, the entity spun around and smacked her with the arm not holding the child's remains. She went down again and the cigarette flew out of her hand and rolled on the floor. My heart sank. Next I knew, Joe Medley was behind me, pushing me forward. "Get the spark," he said in my ear.

I lunged, unthinking, lifted the still glowing butt off the floor, and flicked it. I didn't see it hit, and I was sure it'd missed, but then fire blossomed on the creature's back. In a heartbeat, it had spread to cover the body of the Pariah. Flames leaped to the armoire and in a matter of seconds the tall old closet was a flaming altar. The creature writhed in the flames, but it seemed it wouldn't transform from the physical as long as there was some part of the baby left for it to hold.

Luther grabbed me by the arm and said, "Run." I noticed Maggie and Russell were beside us. Joe Medley was up ahead in the far reaches of the lantern glow, tiptoe jogging like he was running on the moon. The screams of the Pariah chased us up the basement steps and across the living room floor, through which smoke was already rising. We burst out into the night and scrambled for the cars. I went with Maggie and Joe. As we pulled down the dirt road, I looked out the back window of the Galaxie and saw the flames had already reached the porch of the Prewitt mansion.

For the rest of the summer, I lived in mortal dread that the police were going to trace the fire back to one of us. Each day was excruciating. Each day brought a new revelation from the smoldering remains of the mansion—the presence of gasoline, cigarette butts they hoped to get DNA off, tire tracks, and the day they discovered the remains of a small child, identified by a few burnt bones. That was a bad one. I called Maggie, but she told me we shouldn't talk on the phone for a while. We all lay low. I didn't see Russell or Luther for two weeks, and then one night they showed up at my door late with a bottle of cheap bourbon. We sat on the porch in the dark, so no one could see us together, and spoke in near whispers about anything but the killing of Petra.

After that night, another month passed and I saw none of them. I caught a local news report one night, sitting with my father. A delivery man had found an old woman dead in her home. Apparently, she'd died peacefully in her bed, and the coroner believed that she'd probably been gone for two weeks or more when found. The house they showed was unmistakably Marlby Prewitt's. In the end, none of it seemed to pan out for the police. Just in time for me to leave town and head back for my senior year in college, it began to feel like maybe we wouldn't get caught.

Feeling a little braver about venturing out, I walked to Maggie's one night after dark. Knocked on her side door but there was no answer. I went around back to the pool but the place was deserted. Not even Shotsy was there. I made myself a drink at the pool bar and sat down. Scrolling through my recent email, I soon found one from Maggie. She was off to Europe to meet her parents for two weeks before she had to go back to school. I was sorry I'd missed her. The next morning I got a text from Russell. He and Luther were heading back to school a week early.

I felt kind of lonely until I too went back to college. I was worried about the old man, but through the summer he'd made some strides, taken off a few pounds and cut way back on the cigs. He was walking for an hour a night when I left. Somewhere in the middle of the fall semester, during a deep winter snowstorm, I realized something. Maggie had never, as she'd promised, told me "all about it" when it came to her meeting with Marlby Prewitt. I couldn't stop thinking about what had happened in that house, in the final hours of the old lady kept alive by the thing her brain had given birth to.

It was in May, during finals week of my senior year, that I got a call one cool, blue morning while eating breakfast in the university cafeteria.

"I just got off the horn with Russell and Luther," said Maggie.

"Where are you?"

"I'm on a dig. I can't give the location."

"How are you?"

"Great. I love this stuff I'm doing. Hey, have you talked to Russell lately?"

"Not in like six months."

"He and Luther dropped out of school and moved to Brooklyn. They got married."

"What? Those fuckers got married without telling me?"

"Me either," she said. "They didn't tell anyone. I'll text you their address. Send them a wedding present from us and I'll pay you back."

"What?"

"I don't know. Whatever married people get for getting married. An electric can opener, a colander, coasters?"

"I'm gonna go see them this summer," I said.

"Henry, here's why I really called you. I remembered that I'd never given you guys the lowdown on what happened at Marlby Prewitt's place."

"Yeah, I always wondered."

"I went there. This time I knocked and she let me in like she knew I'd be coming. I showed her the bottle of Nepenthe, and she started crying. She was so happy that we were going to destroy Petra and help her die. She'd been in her own prison, alone, for a century. The thing wouldn't let her go; it would never stop looking until it found its child. When Abner Prewitt threw the baby in the outhouse pit, Marlby was in a Nepenthe daze, so the entity didn't know what had happened to Thomas, as Petra had named the boy. The killings were a result of the thing growing so frustrated with its inability to find its baby. I begged her to drink our homemade Nepenthe, but before she did, she confessed to me that even though it had cost her her husband and child and most of her life, she still felt deep empathy for her creation."

I took all this in and my mind reeled with the thought of this whole saga playing out and then being buried by time and night soil and consumed by fire. Only we would know. "Jeez," was all I could get out.

"Okay, gotta call the professor and get moving," she said. "Meet me, July 15, in Brooklyn at Russell and Luther's place. I've got something amazing to show you guys." There was silence.

"Maggie," I called, but knew the line had gone dead. A week later, the address and phone number in Brooklyn came through in a text. I told myself, now that I had graduated, it was time to let my old friends go their own ways and begin the next part of my life, but on the morning of July 14, I found myself in the old man's car, heading south.

About the Author

JEFFREY FORD is the author of the novels *The Physiog-nomy, Memoranda, The Beyond, The Portrait of Mrs. Char-buque, The Girl in the Glass, The Cosmology of the Wider World,* and *The Shadow Year.* His story collections are *The Fantasy Writer's Assistant, The Empire of Ice Cream, The Drowned Life,* and *Crackpot Palace.* His short fiction has appeared in numerous journals, magazines, and antholo-gies, from *MAD* magazine to *The Oxford Book of Ameri-can Short Stories.*

TOR·COM

Science fiction. Fantasy. The universe. And related subjects.

＊

More than just a publisher's website, *Tor.com* is a venue for **original fiction, comics,** and **discussion** of the entire field of SF and fantasy, in all media and from all sources. Visit our site today—and join the conversation yourself.

CPSIA information can be obtained
at www.ICGtesting.com
Printed in the USA
LVOW10s1936230118
563696LV00005B/963/P